West's vision blurred as he looked at his child.

His son.

The towheaded child's little legs pumped like pistons as he ran in circles, his arms outstretched to catch the wind. He was a handsome boy. His hair was as smooth and straight as corn silk. Darkened now with age, West's own hair had been that texture and color once, too.

West had searched for the boy for weeks.

His attention shifted reluctantly from the boy to the striking redhead who was within a few feet of the child at all times. A muscle contracted in his jaw, and his eyes narrowed on her. She was Lesley MacDonald, the woman who'd adopted his son....

Dear Reader,

Our lead title this month hardly needs an introduction, nor does the author. Nora Roberts is a multiple *New York Times* bestseller, and *Megan's Mate* follows her extremely popular cross-line miniseries THE CALHOUN WOMEN. Megan O'Riley isn't a Calhoun by birth, but they consider her and her young son family just the same. And who better to teach her how to love again than longtime family friend Nate Fury?

Our newest cross-line miniseries is DADDY KNOWS LAST, and this month it reaches its irresistible climax right here in Intimate Moments. In *Discovered: Daddy*, bestselling author Marilyn Pappano finally lets everyone know who's the father of Faith Harper's baby. Everyone, that is, except dad-to-be Nick Russo. Seems there's something Nick doesn't remember about that night nine months ago!

The rest of the month is terrific, too, with new books by Marion Smith Collins, Elane Osborn, Vella Munn and Margaret Watson. You'll want to read them all, then come back next month for more of the best books in the business—right here at Silhouette Intimate Moments.

Enjoy!

Leslie Wainger
Senior Editor and Editorial Coordinator

Please address questions and book requests to:
Silhouette Reader Service
U.S.: 3010 Walden Ave., P.O. Box 1325, Buffalo, NY 14269
Canadian: P.O. Box 609, Fort Erie, Ont. L2A 5X3

BABY MAKES THREE

MARION SMITH COLLINS

Silhouette®

INTIMATE™MOMENTS®

Published by Silhouette Books

America's Publisher of Contemporary Romance

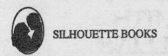

SILHOUETTE BOOKS

ISBN 0-373-07747-5

BABY MAKES THREE

Books by Marion Smith Collins

Silhouette Intimate Moments

Another Chance #179
Better Than Ever #252
Catch of the Day #320
Shared Ground #383
Baby Magic #452
Fire on the Mountain #514
Surrogate Dad #610
Baby Makes Three #747

Silhouette Romance

Home to Stay #773
Every Night at Eight #849

MARION SMITH COLLINS

has written nonfiction for years and is the author of several contemporary romance novels, as well as one book of general fiction.

She's a devoted traveler and has been to places as far-flung as Rome and Tahiti. Her favorite country for exploring, however, is the United States because, she says, it has everything.

She has been a public relations director, and her love of art inspired her to run a combination gallery and restaurant for several years. In addition, she is a wife and the mother of two children.

Chapter 1

West Chadwick, his face like a study in chiseled stone, watched the idyllic scene through a battered chain-link fence. His customary urbane, relaxed appearance, his easy smile, the good-natured sparkle in his light blue-gray eyes, were not in evidence this afternoon.

He'd had a hell of a shock, and he didn't know how he felt about it.

His heartbeat echoed hollowly within his chest, bringing forth unfamiliar feelings. He was not a man inclined toward visceral emotion. Discomfort warred with confusion, regret and—he had to admit—a certain credible pride. He blamed his blurred vision on the spring pollen; his rough breathing, too.

He closed his eyes for a second and just as quickly opened them again. As long as he was here, he didn't want to miss a moment of the scene.

The children's playground was a medley of colorful activity in the picturesque urban park. The day was pleasant, typical of early April in Atlanta. The tulips and jonquils were in full bloom; buds on the azaleas and dogwood trees were filled, ready to burst into glorious color; the grass was neatly mowed.

On its way through the city and across the park, a random breeze lifted and carried the scents of spring. Winding paths, large shade trees, comfortable benches conveniently placed for watching the children—all lent the tranquil ambience to a setting that Walt Disney would have coveted.

As the serenity of the setting was in direct conflict with his own feelings, he was suddenly aware of a contradiction of the sounds, as well.

Before him, on the other side of the fence, high-pitched laughter and gleeful giggles celebrated a sunny day with joyous abandon.

Behind him, the sounds of the city, ignored by the children, were harsh and jarring. The traffic snarled from a few feet away. An ambulance's siren cried in the distance, to be joined by the discordant *whoop-whup* of a police car.

Debris littered the cracked sidewalk. At the base of the fence, crushed cans and fast-food wrappers, dirt and garbage, took refuge in the tall grass that escaped the city's halfhearted attempts at mowing public right-of-ways.

His hands curled in a tight grip around the top bar of the fence, only inches taller than his six-foot frame. A sense of regret intruded somewhere near his heart, adding weight to an already somber burden.

The barrier, designed either to keep the kids in or the creeps out, hadn't been there when he was young. There hadn't been as much traffic on this street back then. Nor were there as many troublemakers, he reminded himself grimly, or as much violence.

A kid used to be able to roam the city without hesitation, to hop a bus from Buckhead, downtown to the Fox Theater for a movie, over to the Varsity for a hot dog and back home, with no thought of danger.

Today's children needed protection. Protection from a lot of things far more dangerous than traffic. In today's world, the six-and-a-half-foot fence more properly should be a ten-foot wall.

West leaned forward slightly from the waist, bringing his face closer to the crimped wire. His paisley tie hung free; his tweed sport coat swung open, revealing a fashionably faded blue shirt, jeans and a lean, fit body. His brown hair would lighten with the summer sun.

Children ran and jumped, slid and tumbled. Their clothes were a bright rainbow—gypsy-rose red, little-boy blue, rain-slicker yellow—picture-book, merry-go-round colors.

Older children sailed sky-high on the swings, pumping with sturdy legs and arms, trying to outdo one another. Younger ones balanced on seesaws, dug in a sandbox and squealed down sliding boards.

West's attention, however, was fixed on the toddlers, who played with balls, pails and spades, and trucks. They watched their older compatriots enviously.

A little girl bolted, running with surprising speed toward more exciting pursuits, only to be chased, collared and detained by her overseer. She merely laughed as though she'd known all along that her attempt to escape was just another game.

Though the play area was crowded, West focused on another youngster, a little towheaded boy in green overalls, a yellow shirt and sneakers.

West had no idea how long he'd been standing there. Staring. He wasn't sure when the regret in his heart grew to an intense pain.

His vision blurred again as he looked at his child.

His son.

Hell. He hadn't cried since he was a child himself and he didn't intend to do so now. He'd never planned on marrying, much less fathering any children. He liked his life as it was. He had a challenging career, lovely, accomplished women when he was so inclined, an extensive group of acquaintances and a few good friends.

He had no room in his life for emotional entanglements. However, the emotion he was feeling now, if that's what it was, did cause him to consider the rightness of what he was about to do.

The towheaded child's little legs pumped like pistons as he ran in circles, his arms outstretched to catch the wind. He was a handsome boy. His head was well shaped; his jaw, determined. His hair was as smooth and straight as corn silk. Darkened now with age, West's own hair had been that texture and color when he was three.

West could discern this child's voice, his carefree laughter, from all the others. He would like to think, also, had he come upon the child unexpectedly, he would have recognized him. But maybe not.

His brow furrowed in frustration. Why hadn't she told him, for God's sake?

Before the question was even fully formed in his mind, he knew the answer. Because he'd always had a certain reputation for not taking relationships too seriously. He'd made it clear—he always made it clear to the women he dated—that there would be no strings, no commitments. But what if he could have helped? What if he could have aided her in some way, avoided not only the three-year-old tragedy but the present quandary in which he found himself? Somehow he knew that the feeling of doubt, the uncertainty, the questions without answers, would be with him for the rest of his life.

West had searched for the boy for weeks. Weeks of dealing with sorrow, seething frustration, dried-up leads, officious bureaucrats.

The search had finally borne fruit two weeks ago today through the efforts of the private detective he'd hired.

Then he'd begun to plan.

From the boy, his attention shifted reluctantly to the striking redhead who was within a few feet of the child at all times. A muscle contracted in his jaw and his eyes narrowed on her.

She was Lesley MacDonald, popular Atlanta personality and anchor of "The Morning News" on Channel Seven, and host of the more domestic, more casual "Lunch with Lesley and Abe" at noon.

Theirs was a sophisticated show, featuring interesting topical discussions with people from everywhere. If they passed through or made an appearance in Atlanta, the producers recruited them for Lesley and Abe.

There was no disputing that she was attractive, perhaps stopping just short of beautiful. But she was more, much more, than merely a good presence for television. In her face were intelligence, talent, self-confidence and a certain spark.

Today, she was dressed casually in wheat-colored slacks and a matching turtleneck. The arms of a darker tan sweater were looped and tied over her flat stomach, and the body of the garment slapped against her thighs as she strolled along self-confidently in the erratic tracks of the child.

Her figure was extraordinary—tiny waist, high breasts and long, long legs. Her lustrous hair, kissed to a glorious shine by sunlight, was short, not quite reaching her shoulders, and neat. A dark auburn—almost burgundy—color, it was cut to frame her face, curving slightly under her chin, moving lightly with a life of its own when she moved and slipping back into its stylish shape when she was still. Her eyes, he knew, were deeply colored, too, but they were blue, a deep, shadowy blue that made him think of moonlit tropical lagoons. She was just the sort of woman to whom West was habitually attracted.

She was also easily recognizable to people in the city and beyond, over most of the state, as well. Her radiant smile, her faultless makeup, were part of her public persona, he thought, even here in the park. He had to admit, however, that she had probably just come from the studio and hadn't taken time to change.

"Oh, look, Billy. Aren't the kids cute? I just can't wait."

The high-pitched voice broke into West's thoughts. He hadn't noticed the young couple arm in arm on the sidewalk behind him. The girl was obviously pregnant. He hardly heard the boy's response.

A jogger ran past; a man with a cane stopped to catch his breath at the corner.

West looked back toward the playground; he gripped the fence more tightly. His conscience gave a slight twitch, but he ignored it. He toyed with the idea of approaching Lesley here and now. Get this situation out in the open, over with, done.

Ah, the hell with her!

His plans were made. He would stick to them. Simple curiosity had led him to the park. The detective had informed him that she often brought the boy here after she returned from the station around one-thirty.

According to the man, Lesley's schedule was rigid by necessity. The light in her bedroom went on at three-thirty in the morning. She left for work at 4:00, went on the air at six and got off work a little after the lunch show was over at one o'clock. On weekends she seemed to spend most of her time with her son.

Today West had just wanted to see the boy; he couldn't wait any longer. That was enough, just to see him.

Enough, for now.

Unnoticed, low clouds had begun moving in over the park. Intermittently, they blocked the sun and began to cast shadows around and among the children.

Nannies and nervous mothers looked at the overcast sky with some trepidation. At the rolling sound of distant thunder, they all began to hurry, to gather their belongings, call to their charges. A chill maligned the benevolent breeze and the smell of impending rain permeated the air.

The redhead lifted the three-year-old boy in her arms. When the child protested, she swung him up and nuzzled his belly until his protest turned to giggles. He was no lightweight, but she handled him with ease. She buckled him into a stroller, looped a string bag of toys on the handle, then she donned her own sweater and started down the path with quick strides.

West watched them leave, admiring, despite his good judgment, the graceful way she moved. He remained in that spot for a long while, staring after them.

At last, he sighed and stepped back from the fence. He became aware of a tingling discomfort in his hands. The heavy fencing had been carelessly cut and lashed to the highest bar with old wire. He looked down at his hands. Streaks of blood lined his palms where the wire had torn the skin. Absently he took a handkerchief from his back pocket and mopped at the cuts.

His gaze swept the area one last time.

Minutes ago, the sun had shone its bright blessing on the city park. Now the overcast was oppressive—like an omen.

And on which side of the fence do you belong, the sunny or the dark? he asked himself.

He had no answer. Not yet.

West and his partner, Luke Quinlan, had their law offices in the northwestern quadrant of Atlanta, halfway between where Luke had built a house for his family overlooking the Chattahoochee River and where West lived alone in a condominium complex.

The decision of where to locate had caused some bickering, but what else was new? Luke and West bickered regularly. However, the men, who had begun as rivals in a prestigious, downtown law firm, had gradually learned to respect each other. Now their friendship, as well as their working relationship, was an unqualified success. But they still bickered.

Besides, it didn't matter where they set up their practice as long as it was convenient to public transportation. Their clients came from all parts of the city. Since pulling out of the huge firm two years ago, they had quickly gained the reputation for taking unusual and difficult cases, cases that other lawyers didn't want to waste time with.

Luke was waiting when West entered the reception room and followed him into his office. "Where the hell have you been? I've got a conference with Davis in fifteen minutes."

West frowned. "So? Hurry up or you'll be late," he snapped.

West's abrupt manner stopped Luke in his tracks—no easy feat. Luke had a will of iron and a jaw to match. But when Luke's face took on that unreadable cast, he could hide his thoughts better than anyone West had ever known. It had been a long, long time since Luke had had to hide his thoughts from West.

West almost smiled at the memory of Lucius Quinlan as he'd been before his marriage to the widowed Alexandra Prescott, before they'd formed this partnership. The changes in the man had been carefully engineered by Alex. And like the changes in West's own life, they were all for the better.

Luke's short-clipped haircut, the button-down collars and conservative ties, the dark suits, the wing-tipped shoes, the overly serious demeanor—they were all vague memories. Replaced—except during appearances in court—by casual chinos, unstructured jackets and cordovan loafers. And his hair was long enough to sit on his shoulders when he didn't wear it pulled tight in a rubber band as he did now to keep it out of his way.

Luke's sixteen-year-old stepson, David, called him "Sully," for his resemblance to a Western character in a Saturday-night television drama.

West sighed. He was fully aware that he wasn't acting like himself, hadn't been for weeks. He was being unfair to his friend and he knew it. He altered his tone and said, "Look, Luke, I'm sorry I'm late. I'll take the Shiffly deposition and the Chalmers hearing."

"The Chalmers hearing has been canceled. They decided to try to reconcile," Luke said, referring to a divorce case. "And the Shiffly deposition has been continued until next week." Luke studied him carefully. "What did you do to your hand?"

The handkerchief was still wrapped around the hand with the deepest cut. "Just a small accident," said West, unwinding the white square and looking at his palms. The cuts were rusty.

"West, something's bothering you. Can I help?"

West laid his briefcase on the desk and stood looking down. "Yeah, something's bothering me, but no, no one can help."

"Try me," said Luke as he dropped into the chair across the desk.

"I have to handle this on my own." West wasn't particularly proud of what he was about to do. He eyed his partner guardedly.

Luke looked as though he were planted in the chair. Clearly he meant to stay until he got answers.

But West knew Luke would give him a fair hearing. Wouldn't he?

Besides, who else was there? Certainly not his parents, and he had no other friends as close as the Quinlans.

Until today Luke had not said a word about the long lunch hours, but West knew that his partner had quietly taken up the slack he'd left over the past few weeks.

It was wrong to expect Luke's support without giving him an explanation. Maybe it *was* time to take Luke into his confidence.

"Okay. Give me a minute." He went into the tiny bathroom off the office and turned on the water. He held his hand under the warm stream, then switched to cold.

The cuts had stopped bleeding, but he gingerly patted his palms dry.

He came back into the office and sat in his chair, facing his partner, wondering where to start.

"Luke." He rubbed a hand down his face and sighed again, heavily. "I know I owe you an apology. I've been acting like more a son of a bitch than usual." He showed his teeth, but what he meant to be a smile was a self-derogatory grimace.

"I'm not complaining," said Luke evenly.

"The story is long and not pretty. It's going to be hard enough to tell. But when we get some free time, I would like to explain it all to you at once, not just in parts." He looked over his cluttered desktop. "If we ever get any free time."

Luke eyed him sharply, then he rose, strode to the open door and spoke to the receptionist. "Betsy, phone Mrs. Davis and tell her I've been unavoidably detained. I'll be there when I can. And please hold all our calls." He didn't wait for an answer but closed the door firmly. "Let's take the time now."

A corner of West's mouth kicked up in a half smile. "Poor Mrs. Davis. She's been good to us."

Sara Davis was a wealthy widow who lived alone. She not only bought and sold property as though it were popcorn, she changed her will every month or so. She'd been one of their first clients when they'd begun the practice, a loyal patron as well as a steady source of income. "Do you think you should keep her waiting?"

"She'll understand." Luke settled in the chair across from the desk again and waited. "Okay. Shoot."

West rested his elbows on the arms of his chair and tented his fingers. "I have a date tonight with Lesley MacDonald."

"The television person? Morning show?"

West nodded. Luke wasn't surprised, but then, why should he be? West enjoyed an active social life.

"She's a good-looking woman, seems talented and smart. I didn't know you knew her."

"I didn't. Caroline Chandler, the woman who owns the station, is a friend of my mother's. I arranged to meet Lesley last weekend at a party at her house."

"You *arranged* to meet her?" Luke's face split into a grin. "Do I smell an infatuation?"

"This might help explain." He opened the top drawer of his desk and took out an envelope. He withdrew the letter it contained and unfolded the single sheet. He looked at the words for a minute, his expression grim, then passed it across to Luke.

Luke's grin faded under the utter seriousness in West's expression and he lowered his gaze to the typewritten letter. He frowned at first—ever suspicious, thought West with an unhappy smile. He could quote the letter from memory:

Dear West,
I hate to have to write this letter. But doctors have discovered that I have a fairly serious cancer, and I'm winding up my affairs. In case things get too bad, I wanted you to know that you and I have a son. He has been adopted by a wonderful woman, who is a perfect mother, and he is healthy and happy. Even she doesn't know who the father is.

This is all I'm willing to tell you. My lawyer will hold this until I'm gone. I've enclosed it in another envelope addressed to him, with the instructions not to reveal any information about the child until he is eighteen; then he will know the whole story and it will be his choice whether or not to contact you.

The only exception would be if the lawyer considers it an extreme emergency. I trust his discretion.

I'm sorry about springing this on you with no warning, but I know you well enough to assume that the last thing you want in your life is a child. And I knew that I would not be a good mother. I will not have our child involved in a "Baby Richard" type of case. That would be horrible for him. Please, West, don't let him go through such a thing. I pray that you will remember the fun we had together and promise me that much. I am sorry—as you can imagine....

Love, Valerie

As he read, Luke's jaw sagged in shock. His astonishment rendered him speechless.

There was a handwritten note at the bottom. The penmanship was shaky:

No feelings of guilt now, West. None of this was your fault. It was my choice. And, as you know, I'm in good shape financially.

West watched as Luke refolded the note. He could almost see the gears turning in his friend's head.

"I don't believe I ever met Valerie."

"No, you wouldn't have. We had a great time together. She left for Egypt or Turkey or somewhere just about the time you married Alex. Or so I thought." He smiled in remembrance. "We weren't deeply in love. She was lighthearted, fun. I liked to be with her. She was smart and independent as hell, liked to travel, was bright and whimsical. The idea that she is dead..." He shook his head grimly. "It's hard to think all that light is gone forever."

"West, I don't know what to say. This is a helluva situation." Luke frowned and his eyes narrowed on his friend. He refolded the note and handed it back to West. "But what does all this have to do with your date?"

West moved his shoulders as though to shrug off his somber mood. "Lesley MacDonald happens to be the adoptive mother of my son."

"Hey, hang on now. First, how do you know?"

"I hired a detective as soon as I received the letter. We've both been working on this for weeks."

Luke muttered a curse. "What are you going to do about it?"

"I don't know yet." West paused, a muscle in his clenched jaw contracting. "I wanted to get to know her, to see if she's really as perfect as Valerie says. If not—" He shrugged.

"Hold it, pal. Didn't you pay attention to the letter yourself? The boy's mother—ah, his birth mother— didn't want you to interfere."

"Then she should have told me she was pregnant," West snapped. "I had a right to know she was having my baby and giving him away."

"But she was right when she said you weren't interested in a child, wasn't she?"

"That's a moot point now. I have a son whether I was in on any of the planning or not. At first I was resentful that she didn't trust me enough to let me in on this. Then, when I really thought about it, I could understand her reasoning."

"Are you going to show this letter to Ms. Mac-Donald?"

"I haven't decided. Probably."

In his urgency, Luke moved to the edge of the chair. "Look, West, don't do anything rash. I'll help you to hash out matters first. This has been a shock. You aren't thinking straight. Why don't you come to dinner at the house tonight? Alexandra might have some ideas or thoughts—"

"Thanks anyway, but I have a date with Lesley tonight, remember? Nope. I've got to look into this personally, then—" a muscle tensed in his jaw "—then I'll do what I think is best."

"This could be a big mistake, West, and I think you know it."

"If so it's my mistake," West snapped.

Luke sighed and got to his feet, sliding his hands into the pockets of his jeans. "I just hope you don't live to regret it," he said softly. He left.

Lesley reached her house just as the first raindrops fell. She tilted the stroller up the steps and manhandled it under the roof of the porch.

The toddler kicked his heels against the frame, throwing her off balance. He was really too big for the stroller, but, living in the city as they did, it was the easiest and safest way to get him from one place to another. "Dallas, quit that."

"Wain! Wain!" he squealed. "Pay in d' wain!"

"Not a chance, big boy."

The door opened behind them. "You barely made it," said an older woman who bent to disconnect the belt that held the child in the stroller. She lifted him out and set him on his feet. "Did you have fun, Dallas?"

He frowned. "No! Pay in d' wain, Newness!"

"Why do you revert to baby talk when you want something, you little mouse?" The woman caught him just as he reached the edge of the porch. "Nope." She forestalled his protest quickly as she lifted him and swung him around. "But you can help make biscuits for supper."

The rain forgotten in an instant, he clapped his chubby hands together. "Oh, boy!"

The women laughed. "You're a glutton for punishment, Eunice," Lesley said.

"I know." Eunice wrestled the cotton sweater off Dallas's arms. "Do you have to go to the potty?" she asked him.

"Yes, by myse'f," he said determinedly, and marched off toward the bathroom.

Lesley folded the stroller and put it away in the coat closet. She shrugged out of her own sweater. "Do you need any help with supper?" She folded and refolded her sweater.

Eunice eyed her curiously. "You know better than that. Are you going to tell me why you're so fidgety?"

"I'm not fidgety," Lesley protested automatically. But she was. Otherwise why would she wait until now to mention that she was going out this evening? She tossed the sweater on the shelf of the closet. "I have a dinner date this evening."

"A date! Wonderful!"

"You make it sound like a miracle."

"Well, let's see...when was the last time you went out with a man? Christmas?"

"New Year's Eve," Lesley corrected with a wry smile. "It isn't easy to find someone who wants to bring a date home at eight o'clock."

Lesley's hours were horrendous. Her alarm went off in the morning at three-thirty, she was dressed and at the studio by four-thirty and prepared to go on the air at six. She worked through the morning and finished her workday with a half-hour news update and interview show at noon with her co-host, Abe Mandina.

But the schedule allowed her to be home by one-thirty or two and able to spend most afternoons and weekends with her son. The arrangement suited her for now. Eventually, as Dallas grew older—well, she would face the problems as they arose.

Eunice snorted. "That's bunk. Most men would overlook your schedule, but it is hard to find one to meet your standards. Tell me about him."

"He's a lawyer."

Eunice kept her expression noncommittal. "A lawyer?"

Lesley laughed. "But he's nice. Really nice. We didn't have a lot of time to talk one on one, but when we did, he didn't treat me as though I were a face." That was her main complaint about the men she met. Few of them could get beyond the fact that she was a television personality.

"His name is West Chadwick. I met him at Mrs. Chandler's dinner party last weekend." The aging owner of the television station where Lesley worked loved to trek out the on-air personalities when she entertained.

Lesley clasped her fingers together, remembering her first encounter with West Chadwick. Her voice softened. "He's charming, interesting. He has a...warmth, I guess you could say, that I liked very much."

Eunice's brows climbed; her eyes reflected her surprise.

Lesley could understand her friend's doubt. She guarded her private life carefully. This eager response and anticipation of a date, especially with someone she barely knew, was quite unlike her.

"What does Mr. Chadwick look like?" Eunice asked.

"He's nice looking, tall, sandy hair. He has eyes..." Her voice drifted off. His eyes were magnetic; she remembered being unable to look away. "His eyes are clear blue, like a glacier."

She stopped, wondering why she had used such a cold comparison. West's eyes weren't cold at all; they were warm and responsive.

"When is he picking you up?"

Eunice's question interrupted her reverie. "What? Oh, at five."

"Then you'd better get a move on." She cocked her head in the direction of the bathroom. "And I'd better check the house for flooding."

Lesley became aware of the sound of rushing water. Dallas thought that washing his hands was great fun.

"Uh-oh." she started toward the bathroom, but Eunice stopped her with a hand on her arm.

"I can take care of it. I just remembered we're low on milk, so I have to run to the market before we can make biscuits. Dallas will want to go with me."

"Naturally." The grocery store was his favorite place. They both had to watch carefully when they took him. He could sneak all sorts of unusual items into the basket.

"You can bathe and dress in peace," Eunice suggested.

"Thanks." Lesley gave her a grateful smile. "That would be heavenly." She watched her friend move down the hall.

"Oh, and wear the black silk," Eunice called over her shoulder.

"Yes, ma'am. If you say so." Lesley watched until Eunice disappeared. She chuckled to hear the older woman's clucking sound that passed for scolding.

Fortune had been beaming on her the day she'd interviewed Eunice Diluent for the position of nanny to her unborn child.

Eunice, long widowed, had one son of her own, a career-navy graduate of Annapolis whose ship was presently patrolling the Mediterranean. When Eunice had applied for the job, she had just turned fifty and admitted to suffering from a case of "empty-nest syndrome." She wanted something to fill her days.

She'd had no professional experience in child care, which had caused Lesley to hesitate. But only briefly.

Like so many women entering the work force today, Eunice had garnered her credentials and qualifications as a volunteer. Besides having reared an exceptional son of her own, she'd donated her time to organizations all over the city.

Her references were astoundingly good, she was clearly intelligent and Lesley liked her right away.

Over the past three years the two women had formed a strong bond of friendship.

Dallas adored "Newness" and the feeling was definitely mutual. Lesley shuddered now at the thought that she might not have chosen this wonderful woman to care for her only child.

Smiling, she listened for another minute to the chatter coming from the back of the house—one special thing she loved about Eunice was that she never talked down to Dallas—then turned and headed upstairs to get ready for her date.

Chapter 2

West pulled his sporty coupe past the ivy-covered stone wall that turned the corner into the driveway. The concrete had buckled in a couple of places from ancient roots and gave his low-slung car a jolt.

Feeling a strong sense of foreboding, he peered through the rain-blurred windshield and the low, dripping branches of a huge old oak tree toward the house. He finally located the break in the wall that indicated a path to the front door.

An older house, Lesley's two-story stucco was the real stuff, not the plastic panels covered with wire and coated with some kind of goop that passed for stucco today.

Huge trees dominated this area of the city, not far from downtown. The district, shadowy even this early in the day, was filled with distinctive old homes. For several years the area had been a favorite with young couples with money to restore, now houses were priced far beyond their original value.

He shook his head. The house and the extensive grounds surrounding it were dark and gloomy. Admittedly the day was dark and gloomy, too. The building's architecture was superior, but the ambience was...well, dismal was the only word that came to mind. The setting looked like something out of a medieval gothic novel. He decided it was certainly no place to rear a young child.

The garage door at the end of the drive was raised. One car, a dark sedan, was parked there. The other slot was empty. He reached into the back seat for an umbrella, got out of the car and dashed through the rain for the front porch.

When the doorbell rang, Lesley felt her heart jump. "I'll get it," she yelled as she quickly climbed the two steps from the hall, black silk skirt swirling around her knees.

There was no response. Eunice had called out a while ago to say they were leaving for the store. Obviously they hadn't returned.

Lesley knew a minute's regret; she would like to have Eunice's reaction to West Chadwick. And, of course, she always loved showing off her son.

She dropped a small flat purse and a white mohair stole on the hall table. Before she opened the door she made one last check in the mirror that hung above the table. No smudged blush, no lipstick on her teeth. She shook her head at her own vanity and opened the door.

"Hi," she said, wishing she didn't sound *quite* so breathless.

West's smile was slow and appreciative, just the thing to boost a woman's self-confidence. Especially one who hadn't dated since New Year's Eve.

"You look terrific," he said. His deep baritone grazed compellingly over her nerve ends. Lesley had forgotten how his voice affected her. She resisted the urge to shiver with pleasure. He looked terrific, too. He wore a beautifully tailored gray suit and crisp white shirt, and his tie was striped with crimson, navy and silver.

His shoulders almost filled the doorway and he was taller than Lesley remembered. It had been a long time since she had met a man who so appealed to her, even longer since anticipation of a pleasant evening with an interesting male had made her feel scatterbrained and silly. She returned his smile. "Thank you. I wasn't sure where we were going so I didn't know what to wear."

"You're just right."

To keep himself from staring at the stunning woman who stood less than two feet away, West looked around the shadowy entrance hall that seemed to bisect the house. This certainly didn't seem like the kind of happy place to rear a child, either. He sought a trivial observation to distract himself. "Your place is—"

Surprisingly, her laughter cut him off. She flipped a switch and suddenly the hall was brightly lit. "Weird, right? I couldn't resist from the moment I saw it. I looked at dozens of houses after I saw this one, but I kept seeing it in my mind as I pictured it finished, like a fairy-tale house." Her eyes sparkled with anticipation. "But I have to take it a room at a time. I've done the living room, kitchen and three of the bedrooms. The entrance hall should be next, I guess, if your reaction is anything to go on."

"No, don't pay any attention to me." West took a step and peered through an arched opening at his left at the living room. "This room is nice."

The room was cleverly decorated, with soft lighting, a muted paper on the walls. He saw comfortable, over-stuffed chairs, a long sofa upholstered in bright chintz, lamps, tables. The far end of the room was unusually rounded and the entire semicircle was made up of un-adorned French doors. If the weather were bright, the room would probably be sunlit and inviting.

"You've done a good job," he said, beginning to re-vise his opinion. But—he reminded himself of his pur-pose in being here—the room was too neat. There were no toys scattered around, no sign of a child at all. Where did Dallas play?

Across the hall an opposing door was closed. Straight ahead the hall narrowed, leading toward another closed door, probably the kitchen area. Stairs with worn car-peting circled, briefly touching the wall to the right be-fore climbing to a balcony. "Are you doing the work yourself?" he asked, doubt clear in his voice.

"Most of it," she declared. "There have been some problems that had to be handled by a professional. I had it completely rewired and the plumbing updated, but the place is structurally sound." She shrugged. "Anyone can use a paintbrush or hang wallpaper."

"Not everyone would try."

"You've seen after. Would you like to see before?" She didn't wait for an answer but slid back one of the pocket doors across the hall.

West eyed the large dark room. Heavy draperies let in almost no light. He could see a fireplace at the far end of the room, the outline of a long table guarded by high-backed chairs. The room was clean but musty smelling. He'd expected cobwebs. "Good Lord. Did the living room look like this?"

She rolled her eyes and slid the doors shut. "It was worse."

He wondered why was it so quiet in the house. He asked.

Lesley laughed. "It isn't normal, I assure you. The nanny has taken Dallas to the store with her."

In this pouring rain? thought West. He carefully kept his expression neutral.

She paused, as though unsure of herself—an affliction that seemed alien to her. "Would you like to sit in here? For a drink of something?" She gestured toward the living room.

He checked the slim gold watch on his wrist. "I made an early reservation at the new House on Peachtree. Maybe we should be on our way. You did say you have to be home before eight?"

"Yes. Unfortunately my alarm clock goes off at 3:30 a.m." She made a face as she picked up a flimsy stole and a small purse from the table. She hesitated. "Is it still raining outside?"

He had reached for the doorknob. Now he looked at her, frowning. Then he brushed at the moisture that clung to his hair. "It's raining pretty hard. You'd probably be more comfortable in a raincoat."

"Good idea." She dropped the lightweight wrap back on the table, opened the hall closet and took out a soft capelike thing, which matched the glossy azalea-pink color on her lips.

He took the cape from her hands. It felt about as heavy as a butterfly. "This will keep you dry?" he asked as he draped the cape over her shoulders. He had a sudden whiff of something floral, something pretty, emanating from her hair.

"Oh, yes." She tied a fluffy bow under her chin, pulled a hood over her hair and smiled up at him. Her creamy, flawless skin glowed with reflected color. Her eyes were clear and framed with the thickest lashes he'd ever seen.

God, why had he ever thought she wasn't beautiful? But it wasn't merely beauty that made him reluctant to look away. She was spirited, vibrant in ways most people were not. She exuded enthusiasm, enthusiasm for the evening out, for him, for life.

"I'm ready," she said.

West recovered quickly and stepped back for her to precede him. This was not a social occasion, he reminded himself. He was here to gather information, not to fall victim to the lure of a charming woman.

The heavy door swung shut behind them with a solid sound. Lesley locked the dead bolt.

He held the opened umbrella over them and walked beside her out to his car. She walked like a dancer, he thought, all fluid movement, from the crisp pace to the gentle sway of her shoulders beneath hot-pink, waterproofed silk.

He shut her door, careful about her cape, rounded the car, tossed the wet umbrella on the floor behind the front seat and climbed in. The well-tuned motor roared to life.

"You say you have to get up at three-thirty?" he asked when they were on the street. "I thought the program began at seven."

"It does, but a lot of preparation goes on before the show starts—the news wires and satellite feeds have to be checked, stories written, the guests, if any, briefed—" She broke off, waving away further explanation. "You don't want to hear all the boring details."

He looked sideways at her and deliberately let his voice drop to an intimate level. "I doubt that anything about you could be boring."

She didn't respond, but a tinge of color climbed her neck. Her eyes darted to him, then away. He saw that she was flustered by the compliment.

Her reaction puzzled him, just as he'd been puzzled when he'd asked her about the quietness in the house. Surely a beautiful woman like this one was accustomed to being told that she was interesting. She was sophisticated enough to take it in stride. Or was she?

Of course she was, he argued to himself. She was a celebrity here in the city. She was poised on camera as well as off.

"I've heard good things about the House on Peachtree, but I haven't been there," she said evenly, as she pushed the hood back to her shoulders and loosened the bow at her throat.

He glanced at her, but could read nothing from her face. Maybe she just didn't *like* compliments.

This evening, planned as an exercise in information gathering, might not be the simple business he'd assumed. But he needed facts on the woman who had adopted his son, before he dropped his bombshell. How had she managed the adoption? Who had handled the legal details? Had she known Valerie personally?

"I haven't been there, either. My partner recommended it," he said at last.

During the rest of the ten-minute drive they talked about other new restaurants and the new growth in the city. Both innocuous subjects...and yet there was nothing harmless about the electricity in the air between them.

At first she'd wondered if she was imagining the undercurrents of awareness. Or if the sensation was all on her side. But a few minutes into the drive, she knew she wasn't imagining. His side-glances held more than mere interest in conversational subjects. There was heat and intimacy in the simmering slate gaze. Exciting, provocative heat.

She closed her eyes briefly. It had been so very long since she'd been affected in this way. It had really happened only once. With *this* intensity.

And that one time had not turned out well, not at all.

A young man met the car at the covered entrance to the restaurant, opened the door for Lesley and gave West a parking voucher. When they entered, a hostess took Lesley's raincoat.

She looked around with pleasure. "This is lovely." Though at this hour the dining room ahead was almost deserted, she glanced through an arch to a lounge that adjoined the room; a trio was tuning up and there was a small dance floor. She followed the maître d' as he snaked through the tables.

The modest name of the place belied the first-class reputation of the chef and the fine decor. Not opulent or excessively ornamented, the dining room, done in shades of rich green and wine, with stark-white accents, was nonetheless impressive.

The table was ready, of course. His table would be ready if the place was packed, Lesley thought.

The maître d' pulled the table out with a controlled flourish, allowing her to settle on a dark-green leather banquette. West hesitated, as though he might sit beside her, but then he took the chair across from her, with his back to the room. The subdued lighting and soft music provided a perfect camouflage for the unfashion-

ably early dinner hour. They might have been enjoying
a midnight supper. By the time they were seated the personal tension seemed to have eased.

A waiter appeared immediately and took their orders
for drinks—Scotch and soda for West and sparkling
water with lime for Lesley.

"Not even a glass of wine?" he urged.

"Not on a weeknight. My schedule really is hectic. I
couldn't keep it up if I didn't discipline myself."

So, she wasn't a heavy drinker; that was a plus.

He smiled into the candle. "You must be disciplined
if you go to bed at eight o'clock. I haven't been to bed
that early since I was five."

She crossed her arms on the table before her and
grinned. The genuine smile activated a dimple he hadn't
noticed before.

"I know, it's awful, isn't it?" Lesley felt comfortable
with him. She wondered how he felt, as she raised one
arm and rested her chin on her palm. "Right now my
son is only three. My crazy hours fit like a glove with his.
But I hope my job changes as he gets older."

"And what would you do if it didn't change?"

His voice had taken on an edge that brought Lesley's
eyes to him. "I don't know," she said after a moment.
"I suppose I'll have to manage that problem when, or if,
it arises." She sat back, withdrawing, and dropped her
gaze to the tabletop.

"What about your ex-husband? Doesn't he help?"

"I don't have one of those," she answered, waiting for
his reaction. She always got one. Sometimes people were
startled, though not so often anymore. Sometimes—
there were still a few shockable people out there—they
looked at her as if she were a bug under a microscope.

Funny, he didn't seem surprised by her pronouncement. "I adopted Dallas something over three years ago."

"Three years," he mused. "I'm sure having a son has changed your life."

"And you're wondering why a single woman would do such a thing."

West didn't want to get into this quite yet. "I don't mean to pry," he said quickly.

She waved her hand dismissively. "Everyone wonders. Some of my close friends thought I'd gone over the edge. But I can barely remember life without him."

"They couldn't have been very close friends. I believe people have to make decisions for themselves."

She thought for a minute, wondering whether it was too soon to reveal intimate details about herself. But there was something about this man that encouraged involvement. "I'll bet you make a hell of a good lawyer."

She actually saw a blush stain his neck; this man of the world was embarrassed by a compliment! The charm of his chagrin decided for her. She looked across the table and into his eyes. She had never made a secret of her background, but neither was it common knowledge that she was a foster child.

"I was orphaned when I was three, just his age now," she told him, surprised at herself, "and I was brought up in foster homes until I was eighteen. After college, I moved from place to place, until a friend of mine got pregnant. She encouraged me to adopt the baby because she knew that my dream was to be part of a family. Dallas—that's my son's name—and his nanny, Eunice, have fulfilled this dream for me. I always know that when I leave, there will be someone waiting for me, someone who cares that I return.''

"A husband could have done that," he offered gently.

"And someday I would like to have that, too. But with my schedule..." She waved dismissively again and let her voice trail off.

"That shouldn't stop a determined man."

"Would you believe I don't even *know* very many eligible men?''

"Not for a minute." He grinned.

She met the smile. "It's true. The ones I work with are all married, and I don't have time to socialize. I'd rather spend time with my son.

"As for Dallas, it's been ... interesting," she said, smiling to herself. "The first couple of years were fascinating—watching him develop, learn to smile and laugh, to sit up and crawl and walk. And talk. Even the 'terrible twos,' as they call them, were fun. Demanding, but fun. He was stretching, testing his limits, testing *my* limits.

"But he had his third birthday a few months ago. This is the best time of all. He's become his own person, with an identity, a sense of humor, a nature that is uniquely his." She shook her head and gave him a self-deprecating smile. "I'm sorry. You couldn't be interested in a discourse on child development."

"On the contrary. I'm exceedingly interested in *this* child."

Lesley responded to West's surprisingly forceful statement with a puzzled look. "You are?"

West cleared his throat and added smoothly, "Because he's yours. Of course I'm interested." He hoped his expression was disarming enough to hide his momentary turmoil.

At that moment, the waiter returned with their drinks. "Would you like to wait to order dinner?" he asked as he set the napkins and drinks before them.

West picked up his menu, indebted to the man for the interruption. "No, we'll order now," he said. He desperately needed to regain control of the situation. He had been taken aback and oddly touched by Lesley's tender description of her child.

Until now West had thought of the boy in terms that related only to him. As *his* son. A son whose existence had been wrongfully kept from him. But, with her short, descriptive sketch of the previous three years, he began to wish he knew Dallas as an individual, too.

The experience was unsettling. And West was not a man to tolerate such an emotion. He didn't know any babies, didn't know anything about them.

The waiter made a few suggestions and they both decided on the grilled salmon. When the man departed, West covered Lesley's hand with his, bringing her gaze back to his face. He was able to smile naturally again; he had recovered his command of the situation. He was here to disarm this woman, to learn her weaknesses, to discover how best to use her love for her son to get his way.

The picture he was drawing of himself was not a flattering one. But then, he reminded himself, he'd been the victim there, not her. He was the one who'd been deceived.

His thumb skipped across her knuckles. "Tell me about yourself, Lesley. I want to know you."

"I've already told you more than most people know," Lesley answered warily. In the past few moments something had happened to change him. She wasn't sure what, but she did know that whatever it was made her uncomfortable. She withdrew her hand under the pretext of sipping from her glass. It was as though he'd flipped a switch; he was once again that effortless, amiable man-about-town. She preferred the man who had blushed at a compliment.

"Are you originally from Atlanta?" he asked smoothly.

"No, I'm from Columbus," she answered, mentioning the smaller city located on the Alabama border. "What about you?"

"Born-and-bred Atlantan. This city is full of aunts and uncles and cousins."

"I envy you. A large family must be fun. Do you have brothers and sisters, too?"

"None of those."

She was trained to interview, to hear nuances in people's voices, and she didn't mistake the hint of animosity she heard in his tone. "Do I detect a problem there?" she asked after a minute.

He looked surprised, then laughed under his breath. "I should have remembered what a sharp journalist you are. You did a good job on my parents."

She stared at him for a minute. Her brows shaped into a frown. "Chadwick...Harold...are you—that's your family?"

West settled deeper into his chair. His expression became almost cautious. "Harold's my father and Christine is my mother."

Christine Chadwick was Atlanta's answer to Paloma Picasso, except that Christine's milieu was fashion, not perfumes. She had recently sold a string of upscale boutiques stretching from Palm Beach to Palm Springs, reportedly for millions. Her husband, investment banker Harold Westmoreland Chadwick II, had sold his brokerage firm at about the same time to a large New York bank. One of Lesley's biggest coups had been an interview with both of them on the occasion of their "retirement."

"Good grief," Lesley said, a bit awestruck. "Are you the third?"

"Don't you *ever* tell anyone that." He grinned. "They tried to nickname me 'little Harold.' When I was about four or five." He shrugged. "Old enough. I refused to answer until they called me 'West', which is bad enough."

"I like West better than Harold, too." She propped her chin on her palm again and studied him. "That house...that was your home?" Her voice rose on the last word.

He laughed, the caution gone, but a tad of bitterness had crept into his tone. "You've seen it. Would you call it a home?"

"It is rather daunting," she conceded, remembering the chill of the huge marble mansion. "I get the impression you don't get along awfully well with your parents," she said gently.

He leaned back, placing his elbows on the arms of his chair, and steepled his fingers under his chin. "Oh, we've always gotten along. We rarely saw each other. But they let me do and have whatever I wanted when I was growing up. Now we see each other occasionally," he stated simply.

"How grim for you."

"It really wasn't that bad. They were both so busy, so rarely at home, that there was no opportunity for conflict. It may sound crazy, but sometimes I envied my friends when they griped about their parents. I longed to overhear a good, rousing argument." He chuckled. "Maybe that's why I studied law."

"So you could hear good, rousing arguments? Do you get many cases with those?"

"Enough. Anyway, my parents were each very successful in their own lives," he concluded.

Leaving a small boy pretty much on his own, she finished the thought for him.

Oddly, she understood immediately what he was feeling. Though her upbringing could hardly have been more dissimilar from his, she, too, had longed for the freedom to be disagreeable.

The kids in the foster parents' program seemed to fall into two major categories: the malcontents and the cheerleaders. The malcontents made trouble wherever they were placed and consequently never stayed in a home very long. The cheerleaders were quietly cooperative. They didn't argue with their foster parents or the other children; they tried to be optimistic and helpful, always hoping that this home would be the permanent one.

For a while, she had been a cheerleader, afraid—no terrified—of the consequences of being labeled a troublemaker. But she'd often yearned for the luxury of arguing with a sibling or protesting a parental decree. She supposed she was a closet malcontent.

Finally, at around age eleven, she had discovered that life wasn't going to get any better, no matter how she behaved. She was an admittedly awful teenager.

"Now that they are retired, don't you see them more often?" she asked him.

They would like that, thought West.

As though, now that they had time for him, he should be grateful for their attention, despite the previous thirty-six years of neglect. He'd played in Little League, high-school football. He could not remember a game, a graduation, any important event in his life, that his parents had attended.

"On holidays, I'm usually invited for a meal," he replied blandly. "If they happen to be in the country."

She didn't know how to respond.

"Listen to me." He shook his head. "I sound like a spoiled, ungrateful brat. I had everything a boy could want. They were just overly busy, occupied."

West looked inward. Actually, he'd recently gotten the insane idea that his parents wanted him to move back into the house with them.

After years of emotional neglect when he was a child, they expected the adult West to behave as though there had never been a gulf in the parent-child relationship. He finally came to realize, after much soul-searching, that in their minds there hadn't been.

At first, in the interests of courtesy and good manners, he tried—though he drew the line at giving up his condo. He went to dinner with the two of them; he appeared at their parties; he talked frequently on the phone with both of them. But he couldn't always control the distance and reserve he still felt toward them—there was no way he could suddenly become an affectionate son to these two people he hardly knew—and they were constantly asking him what was troubling him.

He'd used work as an excuse until it was wearing thin. So he'd decided that a surface relationship was best, and, except for command performances like holidays, he stayed away.

Lesley wasn't offended by his inconsequential answer. His feelings obviously went deep. She found that she wanted to erase the bleak look she saw in his eyes— a look he was probably unaware of. She searched for another subject. "Well, it was certainly a beautiful place to live." The Chadwick mansion, filled with museum-quality antiques and art, sat on nineteen acres of prime Atlanta property in the Buckhead area of the city.

His expression mellowed. "The house is something, isn't it? My grandfather built it. When he was alive..." West's voice trailed off. He didn't try to stem the flood of nostalgia. Laughter had filled the house in his grandfather's day. Laughter that seemed to have died with the old man. He shrugged. "It was different."

"'Something' is an understatement. I didn't see it all, of course. I did the interview—" She waved away her own explanation. "Well, if you saw it—"

"Yes. On the back terrace, overlooking Mother's rose garden. Except that she never planted, sprayed, weeded or even cut the roses. The gardener did that."

Despite his efforts to maintain a mild expression, he knew his closed look was back. He was disgusted with himself for succumbing to the temptation to open up to her. He'd never been one to display his emotions, so why had he told her things that he'd told no one else?

His relationship with his parents was the driving force behind this whole evening. He would not have his son raised in such a sterile atmosphere. No matter what it took. He would stick to his plan.

Their dinner arrived. West deliberately kept the conversation light throughout the delicious meal. When they finished, the waiter cleared the table. Replete, they both passed on dessert but ordered coffee. A comfortable silence settled between them.

Music from the speakers in the lounge had been an accompanying background to their meal, but it halted midsong and a trio began to tune up. The silence between them took on added meaning as the group began to play. A slow, romantic ballad drifted into the dining room, curled around their table. It produced a soothing warmth that wasn't totally welcome.

Lesley looked up to find West's gaze on her.

"Would you like to dance?" he asked.

He took her hesitation for a denial and glanced at his watch. "It's just a few minutes after seven," he offered along with that appealing smile. "Don't worry. One dance and I'll take Cinderella home."

"Cinderella's curfew was extravagant compared with mine," she answered wryly.

The time of day was immaterial. Lesley had hesitated because she was too aware, too drawn by this man. The heat she felt radiating from across the table would surely blister her if she were held close in his arms.

"I'd love to dance," she said, against all her better instincts. "I have to warn you, though, that it's been ages since I danced. Watch your feet."

"Oh, I think I can handle you."

He said it in a suggestive voice, but so low she probably wasn't meant to hear. She pretended to ignore him.

He stood and pulled the table back so she could slide out of the banquette.

Her knees would have been unsteady if she had allowed them to be. But, she reminded herself, this was a first date. One couldn't have genuine feelings for someone one barely knew. Any response, no matter how provocative, was merely lust, and she was far too discriminating to let lust govern good sense.

She paused at the arch when she realized that the small dance floor was empty, but there were other couples in the lounge and two couples rose from their table as she and West entered.

West grinned at her back, his spirits lifting. Maybe his plan would work after all.

Lesley led the way to the small dance floor and turned with a swirl of skirts to face him. The glimpse of her thigh distracted him. He took her in his arms. Her scent was floral and heady, and her body felt warm and light, like thistledown, in his arms. Her breasts brushed his chest, igniting a flare that stopped his breath. Instinctively he tightened his arms.

It was as though a wooden match had flared to life between them. Her head jerked with a start of surprise and she met his steamy gaze. They stared at each other for a long moment.

Lesley felt secluded with him, as though they were encapsulated in a bubble and there was no one else in the room, in the building, in the world. The music, indeed all sound, receded to a background murmur except for the echo of his breathing. And hers.

She could not move away from his heat, his body. She felt melded to him and he to her.

West's eyes took on the blue-gray of a summer storm. He smiled tenderly and guided her head to rest against his shoulder. His hand remained for a second, stroking. Her hair felt like satin, just as he'd imagined. They moved together.

The musicians blended one ballad into a second without a seam. Neither of them noticed.

When the music finally ended, she raised her head, confused by what had happened. Fearful.

He dropped his arms and stepped back from her, to put some distance between them. "Lesley," he said huskily.

Just her name, and her fear became wariness, then alarm. She barely knew this man. She'd never responded like this. Never ever.

"Are you ready?" he asked.

Her fear accelerated. Not fear of him, but of herself. What the hell was wrong with her? "Yes, yes, I'm ready. We'd better be going." Her voice gained strength, thank goodness.

A satisfied smile played around the edges of West's mouth as he took her arm and guided her back to the table. He handed her the small black purse and led her to the door.

He had to admit that he'd been jolted hard, too, as they'd danced. But her response was even more intense.

His plan was progressing nicely.

Chapter 3

By the time West turned into Lesley's driveway, the rain had stopped. Twilight had settled on the damp terra-cotta-tiled roof, giving it a rosy glitter. The house looked slightly more appealing. He noticed a mower, ladder and other equipment that he had missed seeing in the heavy rain. Everything was clustered, and protected by a clear plastic tarp.

It would be a definite improvement, he thought, to trim some of the heavy trees, shrubbery and ivy to let some light into the windows.

But he kept his observation to himself.

The information he was about to reveal would be enough for her to handle tonight. This wasn't the time to criticize her house or her landscaping. He got out of the car and came around to open the door for her.

"Thank you for the dinner, West," Lesley said as they walked toward the front door. She carried the pink raincoat over her arm; her purse was tucked securely in her elbow. "I enjoyed it very much."

The black dress skimmed her slender body. As she spoke she tilted her head and smiled up at him. There was no artifice in her expression, just a soft, warm glow of pleasure. Combined with the too-recent memory of holding her in his arms, it left him suddenly and unexpectedly half-aroused. Damn.

He was familiar with the signs of sensual appreciation for a luscious woman. He had experienced them often enough. She was attractive, alluring; she smelled like heaven and she had a strong measure of charisma. But she was the last woman to whom he could or should be attracted. There were too many complications.

He slid his hands into the pockets of his trousers and looked away. He'd butcher the coming scene unless he had himself totally under control. This situation was too important for him to bungle his explanation.

"I enjoyed the evening, too, Lesley." He took a deep breath and added calmly, "May I come inside for a minute? I know you need to get to bed, but I have something vital I need to discuss with you."

She turned her head to stare at him. "Vital? That sounds serious. I guess you'd better come in."

Lesley was puzzled. Thank goodness, she'd regained her senses on the drive back to her house. What she wanted most was to go to her room alone and think about what had happened on the dance floor. Now he'd thrown her another curve.

West was a complex man—there was no doubt about that; but now he sounded so formal, so stilted and so unlike the man with whom she'd dined and danced.

His expression was unreadable and he'd added nothing about seeing her again. She was irritated at herself for being disappointed. But she refused to believe the electric reaction was all on her side. She'd seen his eyes darken with emotion; she'd felt his arousal.

When they were inside, she gestured him toward the living room. "Have a seat while I check on—on things. I'll be right back." She tossed her rain cape and her purse into a chair as she hurried down the hall. She knew that everything in the house was fine. Eunice always had things under control. But she'd felt a pressing need to escape West's presence for a minute.

As she reached her son's door, she paused. She heard him humming to himself, and smiled. That was his way of falling asleep. She could picture him clearly, lying on his side, his eyes closed, one fist under his rosy cheek.

West watched her go. She paused to listen at a closed door in the hall, then moved farther along until she reached what he presumed was the kitchen area. As she pushed open the swinging door, he heard a radio and someone singing a soft duet with Barbra Streisand.

The nanny. He glanced at his watch. A few minutes after eight. Would a three-year-old be in bed? Hell, he didn't know.

The question prompted another. What did he know about children? Absolutely nothing. Maybe Lesley would bring Dallas out to be introduced. He longed to see the boy up close, but not right now.

That idea made his palms sweat. He entered the living room, straightening his shoulders and buttoning the jacket of his suit as though he was preparing to face a jury. Or a judge.

Now that the time had come to reveal his identity, he was restless and ambiguous. At once, he both dreaded the coming scene and craved the beginning of the complicated process that would allow him to know his son.

He strolled to the far end of the room, the rounded wall of French doors that looked out onto a lovely garden with a swing set and sandbox. Clearly she had done plenty of work here; or someone had, he amended.

When he heard her footsteps approaching from the hall, he removed a folded piece of paper from his inside jacket pocket.

Lesley entered the room and neared the man standing there. His odd expression had not altered. He had a piece of paper in his hand that hadn't been there before. Her heartbeat accelerated as she took the paper he held out. "What's this?" she asked with forced amusement. "Am I being subpoenaed or something?"

His smile held no humor. "No, not a subpoena, a copy of a letter I received a few months ago. I think you'd better sit down Lesley. This will be something of a shock, I'm afraid."

She didn't bother to offer him a drink, or say anything. The entire tone of the evening had changed. While she had no inkling what was to come, she knew intuitively that it wasn't going to be pleasant. She'd learned many years ago how to recognize and face unpleasantness. "What does a letter to you have to do with me?"

She held on to the paper, but didn't unfold it. She felt instinctively that once she did, her life would be changed forever. It scared the devil out of her. But she refused to panic.

"Read it. I believe it's self-explanatory," he said curtly. He stopped when he noticed that her features had taken on the shape of disquiet—brows furrowed, eyes wide, mouth turned down at the corners.

God, he hated this. But he steeled himself. Despite Valerie's plea, he was unwilling to ignore the fact that Dallas was his son. He had to be positive that the child's best interests were being served.

Dallas's well-being and happiness were fundamental to cleaning up the mess that Valerie had left. And the most efficient approach was to tell Lesley, discuss it with her and get into the open any problems that might arise, so a solution could be found.

"Lesley, please read the letter," he repeated, nodding toward the paper. He tried to quiet his tone, be more gentle, but the pressure and tension were getting to him. He looked at the floor. "There's something about your child that you don't know."

"Dallas?"

Her voice rose at the end of the word, but when West glanced up, she showed only surprise, no signs of hysteria. No, there would be no panic. This woman was much too self-disciplined to reveal uncontrolled emotion.

"Please believe me when I tell you, this isn't easy for me, either."

Lesley raised her beautiful eyes, dark as midnight now in her white face. She looked at him questioningly, but his only response was no response.

She opened the paper. Moments later, she felt the air leave her lungs and her head spin dizzily. She knew her heart was still beating because the sound of her pulse reverberated in her eardrums, but she felt so numb that she might have been dead. Long before she finished reading Valerie's words, her hands began to tremble, causing the letter to visibly shake.

"Hell of a situation, isn't it?"

She flinched when the voice, which she had thought was so sexy, turned hoarse. She couldn't bring herself to lift her eyes from the page. She couldn't, wouldn't, look at him. Instead she made herself reread the letter from Dallas's mother. Carefully.

Eventually, the words blurred on the page. "He's dead. Dallas's father is dead." Her voice echoed in her head and she didn't realize she'd spoken aloud.

"Unfortunately he's not," he said dryly. "Valerie lied to you."

Why? For God's sake, why, Valerie? Dallas's mother had been her friend.

Or so she'd thought.

Valerie had *sworn* the father was dead, killed in an auto accident on the interstate between Atlanta and Chattanooga. She'd been very specific.

Now this.

She shoved the letter back into his hands and crossed her arms over her chest, rubbing her upper arms to warm them from the sudden chill that went through her body.

She turned away, wanting to fold inward on herself, and headed for a chair. West followed and sat down across from her.

What could she say? How could she handle this? She refused to cry; she never cried. But for the life of her, she couldn't look at him without wanting to. Tears? Absolutely not, she insisted to herself.

Her vision cleared and fixed on the design in the Oriental rug at her feet. Her voice was almost a whisper when she began to speak. "I met Valerie when I was working on a story about private adoption agencies. We became immediate friends."

Valerie Palmer had been unlike most of the mothers-to-be. For one thing she had been older—twenty-six. She was enjoying her pregnancy; she was intelligent, fun to be around. Lesley's gaze, still on the rug, traced the burgundy curve of a golden bird's tail.

The moment of reflection had calmed her. At last she raised her eyes to the man who sat across from her. "She told me that she had never entertained the idea of abortion, but she had no intention of keeping her child. She felt that someone who really and truly wanted a baby would be grateful to her."

"Why you?" he asked. "I would have thought she'd want the child placed with a family."

Lesley's chin tightened to a determined angle. "Dallas has a family. It may not be a traditional father and mother, but he couldn't possibly be more loved. And that's all I intend to say on the subject right now."

"That's bull. We have a lot to talk about. Postponing it won't help."

Lesley shook her head; she fought off a feeling of helplessness. "Why are you doing this to me? Why now? Tonight?"

He didn't answer.

"In case you don't recall, the news is my business. I am fully aware how the courts have ruled on this subject in the past. As a lawyer, you are even more conversant." She lifted her arm to rake the shining hair back from her face. "I have to have time to think this over, maybe consult my own lawyer."

As she spoke, his expression grew glacial. "I was hoping that if we talked about this, it wouldn't go so far as the courts." He shrugged. "But if that's how you want it . . ."

In a way it was good that he was cold. His attitude fueled her anger toward him. "You lied, too, you know," she accused coolly.

He leaned forward, resting his forearms on his knees. "I don't deny that, and I'm not particularly proud of myself. My only excuse is that I wanted to get to know you before I sprang this on you."

She shook her head slightly. "Yeah, sure," she said, smiling humorlessly.

She had never misjudged anyone so completely. She almost laughed aloud. She'd liked him so *much;* she had been ready to name West Chadwick Atlanta's Man of the Year or some such. She'd genuinely liked his smile, his intelligent eyes, liked *him.*

It hurt that she had opened her emotions a crack, and was so wrong. And it revealed what a fool she had been.

Well, not anymore. She now had the good sense to recognize that he was her enemy.

Her vision clouded with anger. "It seems that we have a gigantic problem here," she said huskily. And she saw, distinctly, the blank expression of the dishonest, deceitful, manipulative son of a bitch. He was looking at her seriously; surely he couldn't mean—

Fury gave her the stamina she needed to get through the next few minutes. She schooled her features and stared straight into those glacier eyes. "Dallas is my son. I adopted him as soon as he was born," she said, her voice steady and even.

"He's also my son, and I didn't know of his existence. The letter verifies that. I have the right—"

"He's *my* son!" She surged to her feet, but her voice was equally controlled and cold. "We'll see about your rights."

His smile was frigid, to match the winter evening sky of her eyes.

That was the last straw. She glared at him. "Get out of my house," she snarled. "Now."

"We'll have to talk about this situation sooner or later, Lesley."

She rose and started toward the front hall, her carriage as straight as a rod. "Let's make it later, shall we? You know my rigorous schedule, and right now I want you gone."

He followed her to the door. She opened it and stood waiting, but he paused on the threshold. "Lesley—"

"Get out," she said in a low voice. "Now." Another minute and she would lose herself. She would be screaming at him.

He looked at her for a long, tension-filled moment. And left.

Lesley closed the door carefully and locked it. Moving like an automaton, she traversed the hall to Dallas's room. She opened the door, crossed the room, sat in the rocking chair close to his bed.

He was lying on his stomach, his bottom in the air. She rocked slowly and watched her baby sleep.

It had been Valerie's idea from the start, something thrown out as a sort of "what if".

Valerie knew Lesley's background in foster homes, sensed a need in her for stability and made her face it.

Valerie's arguments had surprised her, opening her eyes. Lesley had kept her focus so earnestly on digging out of the deep hole that was dependent care that she was missing a lot of the wider and more expansive aspects of life. She had amassed hefty bank accounts, and though she wasn't ready for retirement, she could afford to enjoy life without apprehension.

Lesley was not certain when she had first begun to accept the thought of adopting Valerie's child.

She had dismissed the idea initially. Her independence was hard won, had taken her years to achieve, and she had no intention of giving it up.

But over the weeks and months, and under Valerie's compelling encouragement, the notion had grown into conjecture, then into final, unshakable certainty that adopting was the right thing to do.

Moreover, it was what she *needed* to do.

Lesley MacDonald had always wanted a family. She'd always wanted to belong to someone and have someone belong to her.

She'd never known her parents, she'd never known the love and companionship of brothers and sisters. She was a product of the uprooting, undependable, uncertain foster-care system. She realized, looking back with an adult eye, that she had been a very difficult adolescent. Even then she'd been self-sufficient, afraid to let herself care for fear of another disappointment.

When she'd skinned her knee, she'd never gone to an adult to have it kissed and made better. When she'd been ridiculed by other children as a foster child, when she'd been excluded from birthday parties, she hadn't had an understanding adult to explain and sympathize with her feelings.

She had simply decided that was life, and she had better learn how to deal with it on its own terms. So, throughout the years, she'd buried her emotions deeper and deeper, until they were almost totally hidden.

She didn't like to think about those childhood years when she'd lived in seven houses in ten years. After that point she had stopped counting.

When she was eighteen, she had walked away from being a ward of the state. She had determination, a well-thought-out plan for survival, and she hadn't looked back.

Her grades had always been exceptional. She'd worked her way through college and, off and on, grad school. She'd striven mightily to reach a level of success solely on her own merits.

Now she was proud of what she had achieved. But her struggle to pay for her education had put her several years behind her peers. She had just begun to catch up.

Lately there were even trial feathers in the wind, tentative ones to be sure, but small hints—of a move to New York. To the network.

She clenched her fingers into fists. Her friend Valerie had not only been a liar, but a remarkably creative and accomplished one, she thought bitterly. Deceptive throughout the pregnancy, and afterward.

Lesley had made a concerted effort to be supportive and caring. Despite her own harrowing schedule, she'd tried to keep Valerie occupied and entertained. She took her friend shopping, out for meals, to movies and the theater, boosted her spirits as her stomach swelled and getting around grew more difficult. They'd laughed together when Valerie had compared herself first to a grapefruit, then a pumpkin, then a dirigible.

And all along, Valerie had pretended to a sadness that had been a horrible, heartrending lie.

Lesley had been lied to before. Often. She despised it.

She rose and started to pull the blanket over Dallas, but instead she lifted the sleeping child in her arms and sat down again in the rocker she'd used when he was a baby.

He nestled close. She felt his warm breath on her neck. He smelled like baby shampoo. Tears ran silently down her cheeks. Her hand shook slightly as she smoothed the soft, blond hair off his forehead and placed her lips there.

"No one is going to take you away from me," she vowed in a fierce whisper against his skin. "No one!"

Outside, the rain had begun to fall once more.

West gripped the wheel until his knuckles were white.

He was in a turmoil. He didn't want to go home. He snorted—

Home was a condo, decorated by the best designer in Atlanta, but it had no heart. Home should have heart.

He was tempted to head for Luke and Alexandra's house, but he quickly vetoed that idea. Luke had warned him that he'd be opening up a can of worms if he intended to pursue this. He'd find no sympathy there, not that he deserved any.

Luke was right. What had he started? And where did he go from here?

He was going to have to execute some damage control immediately. He needed to talk to Lesley again. To hide his own anxiety, he had come on like a prosecutor.

He'd bungled the whole evening. Not until he'd looked into her eyes, beyond her controlled expression to the vulnerability hidden deep there, did he realize how badly he'd bungled.

That night, Lesley's sleep spawned a familiar nightmare for the first time in years. Her mother—hiding from her, dismayed when she saw Lesley, running away. The dream was preposterous; she'd never even known her mother.

The next morning, she went through the wire stories, did some writing and consulted on the schedule for the morning with her cohost, Abe Mandina, and their producer, Blanche Tolland. The strain of doing a morning news show was in the immediacy of the news itself. Flexibility and improvisation were the keynotes of a good host. Abe, a number of years older than she was, and aeons ahead in experience, was a pro.

A tall, medium-toned black man, Abe didn't bother to cover the rapid graying in his hair, as so many of his peers did. And as it did his conscientious temperament, his face reflected his trustworthiness. He was blessed with a beautiful, if rare, smile. She was fully aware of how lucky she was to have received this slot, and had learned a lot from being paired with him.

It was a heavy news day, and they had breakaways to New York, L.A., London and the Mideast; so they had rescheduled the two guests they'd planned to interview—one, a rock star in town for a week of concerts at the Georgia Dome; the other, a prominent economist who had settled in the city and promised to come again whenever they needed him. The rock star was a little more touchy, but he finally acquiesced.

They had finished blocking out the show, when Abe and Blanche both turned to her.

"You aren't yourself this morning. Something's happened," stated Abe flatly. "Do you want to tell us about it?"

"You look like hell. Is it Dallas?" Blanche added. "Is he sick?"

Lesley hesitated. She'd known this was coming. These two were her closest friends. They'd both given her long, steady looks when she'd walked into the building at 4:15. She was rarely even a minute late.

But at that moment the director's voice had boomed out from above, a telephone rang and the fax had begun to spit out a document.

Abe paused with his hand on the phone; Blanche spoke into her headset to the director. Both of them still looked at Lesley expectantly.

She would like nothing better than to unburden herself to her friends but clearly now was not the time. "Dallas is fine. It's—something else." She folded her hands on the table, littered with coffee cups and crumpled memoranda. "I'd really appreciate your opinion on a problem that's come up, but it's a long story. We don't have time for me to go into it now. After the show?"

"Sure," they answered in unison. Abe picked up the persistent phone. Blanche waved her off. "We'll meet in my office at one o'clock. You'd better let Roy get busy on you anyway."

Lesley gave a halfhearted grin and rose. "That bad, huh?"

"Pretty bad," Blanche teased with a grin.

Abe put his large hand over the telephone receiver and gave her a glimpse of his smile. "Scat. We'll finish up here."

A short time later, Lesley apologized to Roy for her appearance. She dressed at home—today she wore an aquamarine blazer with a simple white blouse and gold choker—but Roy did her makeup and hair for the show each day.

"I had trouble falling asleep last night," she told him, wondering if he would accept such a blatant lie. She examined her face critically in the mirror. There were shadows under her eyes and her lids were puffy from the self-indulgent tears she'd shed after West had left.

And from the nightmare.

But this morning the tears were gone, replaced by a glint of determination in her eyes.

"Don't apologize," Roy chided.

She watched his reflection as he laid out his instruments of embellishment—pots of color and soft, sable brushes; delicately shaded pencils and translucent powder; curling irons and sprays.

"It's nice to know you're human."

She touched a toe to the floor, turning the chair to face him. "What?"

"You never have bad nights like Paige and Abe," he said, mentioning her cohost and the sports reporter. "Doing you is no challenge."

She laughed at this, as she was meant to, and the look of the tension disappeared from her face as if by magic. Her lips relaxed as she turned back to the mirror.

Roy flipped a navy blue cape over her shoulders to protect her clothes and tied it at her nape. He leaned over her shoulder to examine her face for himself. "That's better," he confirmed.

"Abe and Paige have bad nights, huh? You want to share some of this information with me?"

"And have my neck wrung when you razz them? Not a chance."

When Roy was finished, all traces of last night's bitter scene and its aftermath were gone. "You *are* a miracle man," Lesley said, turning her face this way and that, searching for signs of the tears she'd shed last night.

"I know," he said without conceit. "Just don't test me too often."

"I won't. Promise."

He smiled approvingly at the determination in her voice and the smile that curved her lips. "Great. It wouldn't be good for the ratings if our early-morning hostess looked unhappy on camera."

Roy removed her cape and Lesley headed for the set.

She kept the smile in place. "Good morning," she said briskly to Carl and Paige, the weather forecaster and sports announcer respectively. She was certain that neither of them noticed anything wrong.

Lesley paced the length of Blanche's office and back. She had described the scene in her living room with West last night, omitting her feelings during dinner and the electricity that had sparked between the two of them as they'd danced.

"I don't know what to do next. I realize that I made a tactical mistake in throwing the bastard out." She rubbed her bare arms. They had all shed their suit jackets along with their professional images when they had entered Blanche's office earlier. "But Dallas is *mine*. Mine. It isn't fair."

Abe and Blanche exchanged a look. Both were familiar with past custody-battle news stories, the long trials going all the way to the Supreme Court, which so far had always come down on the side of the natural parents. They remembered the frantic wrenching of children from the only homes they had known; the tears and screams of one child as he was pulled away from his adoptive mother.

Blanche propped her elbow on the arm of her chair and covered her eyes with her fingers.

Abe slowly shook his head. When Lesley passed him he reached out and snared her hand. "Sit down," he ordered. "You're making me nervous."

"How do you think I feel?" she snapped, but she sank into the chair beside him, facing their friend across the desk.

"The first thing you've got to do is get a lawyer of your own," said Blanche, straightening in her chair.

"The best we can find. A big gun. I'll talk to our legal department."

"You do need professional help," Abe agreed. "But you don't want to alienate this man. He's a lawyer, remember. With a good reputation."

"You know him?" asked Lesley.

"I met him once, years ago. But I know of him. I met his partner, too—Luke—something." He shrugged and went on. "They were both with one of the big silk-stocking law firms downtown until three or four years ago. But the story goes that they got tired of seeing how many billable hours they could generate. They decided to get out, to practice their own kind of law. They've helped out a couple of friends of mine, small business-men no one else wanted to fool with."

Lesley stared at her friend. He made West sound like a paragon of virtue. Then she remembered that she had liked the man, too, until he'd sprung Valerie's letter on her. "Liked" was too tame a word for what she'd felt last night as they'd danced. She felt heat rising in her face. "Why didn't he just call me, or arrange a visit? Why the deception of asking me for a date?"

Abe shrugged again; he avoided her eyes. "It's one way of arranging a meeting, isn't it? He asked you to have dinner with him."

"Whose side are you on?" she demanded, crossing her arms in an quick-tempered gesture. But she didn't feel as angry as she did frightened.

"Yours, of course," he said gently. He leaned forward and touched her crossed arms briefly. "But I also want you to be aware of the difficulties you're facing."

"You don't sound like you're on my side," said Lesley, calmer now.

Blanche had been silent during the exchange, but now she spoke up. "We're both on your side, Lesley. You know that. But we're trying to look at this objectively."

Lesley's shoulders curved in defeat. "I know," she said, trying unsuccessfully to keep the emotion out of her voice. "And I know that this could become long and complicated. I have a lot to think about."

"Well, the first thing is to get a lawyer," Blanche reiterated briskly.

"There's another problem," Lesley added. "This was a privately brokered adoption."

They looked at her, not understanding.

"You remember the private adoption agency that I investigated when I was doing consumer affairs?" Lesley asked, referring to the position she'd held before she'd been promoted to morning anchor. "Well, the adoption was handled by them. The Georgia Department of Human Services had nothing to do with it. The paperwork was all done by the private agency and their lawyer." She paused, anxiety shadowing her eyes. "Now I wonder if I made a mistake not insisting on knowing the name of the father."

After a minute Abe spoke. "I doubt that you should worry about the legality. I've often heard about private adoptions that have no complications. My concern is that the father wasn't told he had a child until now. Wasn't Dallas's mother a friend of yours?"

"Valerie is—was—a very good friend." She shook her head. "I still can't believe she's dead. Anyway, she assured me that the baby's father had been killed in an accident on the interstate between here and Chattanooga. As for the legality, I had investigated that agency myself for a story, so I had no qualms about using them."

Blanche moved to rest her elbows on the desk. "So, Valerie lied. Or, this man says she lied."

"I saw a copy of the letter she wrote to him. She acknowledged what she'd done. She didn't tell him who I was, just that the baby had a good home.

"I am sure that the caseworker who handled the adoption wouldn't reveal my name. John Conniers is a dear," she added, her voice and expression softening at the thought of the kind, jolly man.

He had been wonderful throughout the process, never forcing his opinion on Valerie or demanding any quick decisions from Lesley. They had both appreciated his caring attitude; as a matter of fact, she had sent him flowers as soon as she'd received the final papers. He'd called her immediately to thank her. He said no one had ever sent him flowers.

"Chadwick must have had a damned good detective," said Blanche musingly.

"I'd like to say that Valerie had no idea he would even try to find the baby. From what she told me, their affair was short-lived. But now that I know what a masterful liar she was—" Her voice broke.

"I've seen her handwriting many times," she added, before her friends could ask. "And I knew the way her mind worked. She wrote the note."

Chapter 4

The conversation in Blanche's office had delayed Lesley's getting home. It was almost three in the afternoon when she pulled her car into the driveway. She was gratified to see that two men were working in the front yard, one on a ladder, pruning the trees; the other man, edging the walkways.

The ivy had been trimmed away from the windowsills—they would have to be washed again—and tamed along the walls. All in all the large area looked much more welcoming. She smiled to herself. As if someone cared about the place.

The feeling that had drawn her to the house in the first place, and kept bringing her back, was the atmosphere of apologetic abandonment. Almost as though the house were speaking to her: "Here I am. I know I don't look like much at present, but I could sparkle and shine if someone cared enough to polish me up a bit." A whimsical impression of a house in which to invest her hard-earned money, but she'd never been sorry.

Moving forward into the garage, she felt the same anticipation she felt every day when she came home. Someone was waiting for her, someone special. She had a family who cared about her. A time might come when she had to remind herself of the importance of that.

She refused to look further into the future.

She determinedly put aside the twinge of her earlier fear. The discussion with her friends had been a sort of catharsis for her. They'd given her some good advice, and some that she'd have to think carefully about.

Right now, she needed to stay focused on this small family, their love and their needs.

She switched off the ignition and gathered up, along with her purse and jacket, several file folders containing background information on her interviews for the next few weeks. She planned to spend a part of the weekend studying. In this job one had to stay ahead, because there were always important, unexpected stories cropping up.

Dallas met her in the back entrance hall, his grin wide and his blue eyes shining bright enough to light a night-time sky. "I wondered why you was late, Mommy. But here you are."

She dropped the things she was holding onto a chair and scooped him up for a big hug. "Here I am," she agreed, letting him lean back, but with a strong hand at his back. "And it's the weekend. I have two whole days. What are we going to do first?"

"Go to the zoo!" he squealed without hesitation. He loved the Atlanta Zoo, located in Grant Park, almost as much as he loved the rain. "Can we, Mommy?"

"Sure. We'll go as soon as I change my clothes. Do you think Eunice will want to go with us? We could pick up a pizza on the way home."

"The zoo and pizza!" said Dallas, elated.

Eunice seated at the kitchen table, chuckled under her breath as she shook her head.

Dallas put both hands on Lesley's cheeks and turned her face back to his—his way of obtaining her undivided attention. His smile was gone and he wore his earnest look. "But Newness might wan' a rest from me," he said seriously.

"Uh-oh," answered his mother. "Have you been difficult today?"

The child, clearly seeing his trip about to be canceled, shook his head vigorously. "No, no, no. I jus' heped the men outside. Can we still go to the zoo?"

"May we," she corrected automatically. Since her child was all in one piece, Lesley wasn't really concerned, but she raised an inquiring brow toward Eunice.

"We went out to tell the men what you wanted done." She indicated the list Lesley had left pinned by a magnet to the refrigerator. It had been crumpled and smoothed out again. "This little monkey was up the ladder and crawling out on a tree limb before any of us knew it. But the only harm done was to my blood pressure."

"I'm a monkey," Dallas said, laughing. He squirmed to be released and Lesley set him down. He ran to Eunice and plopped his elbows in her lap, looking up. "Like the monkeys in the zoo?"

"Exactly like the monkeys in the zoo," she told him, ruffling his hair. "Maybe faster."

"So you've had enough monkeyshines for one day?" probed Lesley. The older woman appeared tired.

Eunice smiled. "If you don't think you'll need me, I have some letters to write."

"I think—I hope—I can handle him alone for a few hours," Lesley said dryly.

When Eunice had first come to live with them, Lesley had made sure the older woman knew that her weekends were free. A few times she had spent the night with friends, but aside from her son, the only relatives she had were a sister and brother-in-law who lived in Virginia.

After only a few weeks, a familial warmth had grown between the two women. Eunice decided she'd rather stay here most weekends. "You're the closest thing I have to family within four-hundred miles," she'd declared. "If I won't be in your way—"

She'd never finished the statement. Lesley had hugged her—tight. "This is your home, too. We want you with us whenever you want to be."

Eunice still visited with her old friends whenever she felt like it, and occasionally she took an overnight trip with them. But most weekends she came home to the small apartment Lesley had fixed up next to Dallas's room.

"Okay, the zoo it is. We'll give Eunice a rest for the afternoon." She picked up the things she'd dumped on the chair and started out of the room, only to be stopped by Eunice clearing her throat.

She turned back, a quizzical smile on her face.

"While we were outside this morning, a message was left on your answering machine."

Lesley could tell that Eunice didn't want to say more in front of Dallas.

"Sweetheart," she said, "I'll have to change before we can leave. Why don't you find my sneakers for me? They may be under the bed." The sneakers were in the closet, where they belonged, but it would take him a few minutes to figure it out.

"Who was it?" she asked as soon as he was gone.

"West Chadwick. I take it the evening didn't go well."

"You could say that," said Lesley. She had no secrets from this woman, but it wasn't as easy to talk to her as it had been earlier with her more objective co-workers. She knew that Eunice's reaction would be as emotional as hers had been.

"He apologized," Eunice offered. She waved toward the machine on the counter.

Lesley pushed the button to replay the message. The deep, familiar baritone provoked no warm reaction in her this time. Instead she tasted bitterness and aggravation on her tongue at the sound.

"Lesley. This is West. If you haven't hung up on me by now, I want you to know how sorry I am for the way we parted last night. I handled...things...clumsily and you had every right to ask me to leave. But we're both adults and I hope you'll allow me to try again. May we meet? Have dinner again and try to work out our problem? I'll wait to hear from you." She stood for a moment, totally still, and listened to him give two numbers: one he identified as his office; the other, his home. The machine launched a piercing, but blessedly short, tone through the room and clicked off, leaving them in heavy silence.

Lesley's first inclination was to call him back immediately and tell him to go to hell. But, in addition to her animosity, she couldn't completely erase the memory of those court decisions, the children on television, the microphones being shoved in their parents' faces, their screams of fear at the wrenching conviction that they were being rejected by those they loved.

The images haunted her.

It was as though two opposing magnets were warring within her chest, pulling her first one way and then another.

Last night after she'd put Dallas back in his bed, when she'd finally washed her tear-streaked face and stumbled to her bed, she had lain awake for a long time, first cursing West, then Valerie, then fate.

At last, just before she finally fell asleep, she let herself think about all this from his perspective—his surprise at learning that he had a child, his sentiments on being a father. She had to admit that she hadn't given him a chance to voice his impressions, his emotions.

West's masculine appeal was dangerous. She'd recognized that early on. But so was his rancor. What would she do if he pushed her on the subject? Or demanded custody?

She had acted in good faith, and so had the adoption agency. But, from what she understood, good faith didn't amount to a hill of beans when the father of the child had no knowledge of his existence.

Suddenly she turned to Eunice, who had waited quietly for her decision. "Would you do me a very large favor?" she asked.

"Of course," answered Eunice without hesitation.

"After we've left for the zoo, would you call him for me?" She could see Eunice's protest forming on her lips and she went on hurriedly. "Please. I can't talk to him yet. Just say that Dallas and I will be having pizza at that new place on Peachtree close to Piedmont Hospital at— oh, say six-thirty—if he wants to join us there."

"Are you going to tell me what's going on?"

"Tonight, when we get home. I promise."

Eunice thought for a minute. Her kind eyes turned stubborn and Lesley knew what was coming.

"Under one condition," she announced flatly. "Somewhere around seven o'clock, I will also be at the pizza place. In that case, if the two of you get into another argument, I can bring Dallas home."

"That's perfect," said Lesley, giving the older woman a hug. Eunice always had Dallas's best interests foremost in her mind. "You are a dear. I wouldn't have asked, but thanks for suggesting."

"Mommy!" Dallas's angry voice reached them, but it sounded far away and slightly muffled. "Come to Dallas!"

Both women started for the door to the hall. "Oh, dear, he's still under the bed," said Lesley.

He wasn't simply under the bed; he was stuck. And not too happy with either of them when they laughed.

West stood near the glass door of the recently opened pizza parlor, watching the traffic speed by on Peachtree Street, waiting impatiently for his first close-up glimpse of his son.

His son. His genes, his DNA, his own son. The idea was overwhelming. He shoved his hands into the back pockets of his jeans and his chest expanded with some emotion akin to pride.

Then his shoulders sagged; his hands fell to his sides. Hell, what did he have to be proud of? A defective condom and a woman who decided against abortion. A few months ago he hadn't even known the child existed.

He looked at his watch. He read 6:28. He was eager. But he fidgeted, at the same time dreading the imminent meeting. What if the child took an instant dislike to him?

He practiced a smile on the hostess.

The hostess smiled back, but she had a puzzled expression in her eyes.

He realized that though his mouth curled and his teeth were showing, the rest of his face was as stiff as a board. His expression was probably more of a troll's grimace than a smile.

He shouldn't have come, he thought suddenly. This was too quick.

Lesley was furious with him—appropriately so. He'd been insensitive and heavy-handed. Her resentment toward him would surely communicate itself to the child. The kid was sure to take one look at him and start screaming. He would have been much wiser to wait until he and Lesley could meet alone again, talk and try to smooth over their disagreements in a reasonable manner.

He knew that today's women demanded sensitivity in a man. Didn't they?

West was pretty good at bluffing. Truth was, he didn't know a whole lot about women except how to please them socially and sexually.

His mother hadn't been a particularly good role model. She had been a successful career woman who was perfectly content to leave the care of her child to others. He'd never really gotten to know her during the years of his childhood and adolescence. She hadn't been around all that much.

Maybe he should leave.

He looked at his watch—6:30 on the dot. Oh, hell. He took a step toward the glass door.

Too late.

He held the door open for the woman and child as they approached.

"Good evening, West," said Lesley evenly. "I hope we haven't kept you waiting long."

He deliberately kept his gaze on hers, almost afraid to look at the child. "No. Thanks for letting me meet you." He was caught in her midnight-blue eyes. Today she had on no makeup. Her nose was pink, as though she'd been in the sun. She, too, wore jeans and a casual shirt, the color of tree-ripened peaches.

Lesley seemed unable to tear her eyes from his. She wondered vaguely why in the world she'd ever thought this was a good idea. Her reservations about sitting down across from this man again so soon returned with a rush.

"Mommy, you're squeezin' too hard," said the toddler at her side, twisting his hand within hers and eyeing West suspiciously.

She held on, but she looked down absently, as though she'd forgotten the child was there. "I'm sorry, sweetheart."

West tensed. Then he nodded to the hostess, who led them through the restaurant packed with children, parents and teenagers. They finally reached a booth in the back, where the noise level was slightly more tolerable.

"Are you going to introduce me?" he said when they were seated. He was on one side, alone; she and Dallas on the other.

Before she could speak, West smiled and held out his hand, palm up. Wasn't that how one approached unknown entities? "I'm West Chadwick, and your name is . . . ?"

Dallas was on his knees, next to the wall, penned in by his mother, who remained silent. He hooked two fin-

gers over his lower front teeth and looked from the
man's face to the big hand for a long minute. Then he
turned his serious gaze back to the man.

His eyes were beautiful, thought West, amazed at their
clarity. They were sky blue and guileless. Lashes that
seemed as soft as dandelion fluff curled up toward his
light brows.

West held his breath.

At last Dallas removed the fingers from his mouth and
tentatively laid his hand in West's. "I'm Dallas Mac-
Donald," he said with a shy smile.

Oh, God.

A huge lump formed in West's throat. He shook the
hand gently, wet fingers and all. "How do you do, Dallas?" he said, the lump roughening his voice.

"Well-l-l, I'm really hungry," Dallas answered honestly, breaking off the emotional moment.

West was relieved. He'd been ready to... what? Cry?
Surely not.

Lesley took a deep breath and let it out. She smiled at
West. "I'm hungry, too," she said lightly. "Dallas and
I spent the afternoon at the zoo."

"Yes, Eunice told me."

"Do you know Newness, too?" asked Dallas. "She
takes care of me when my mommy has to work on TV."

A shadow crossed West's face. Lesley saw it clearly,
but she had no idea of the cause.

"I talked to her on the telephone," West said, sum-
moning up an easy smile for the boy. "She sounds very
nice. Do you like her?"

"Oh, no, I *love* Newness. That's bigger than like."

West chuckled. "You're right. Much bigger." He
looked at the young woman who was waiting to take

their order and then at Dallas. "What's your favorite kind of pizza?"

"One with everything."

"No," said Lesley, eyeing him fondly. "I have no intention of being up all night because you have a tummy ache." She poked him in the named spot and he giggled.

West stared, envying them their easiness with each other. He could never remember his mother poking him in the stomach to make him laugh. Or looking at him fondly for no particular reason.

Lesley caught the bittersweet smile on West's face as he watched Dallas, again wondering what caused it.

She shook herself. She was not going to feel sorry for this man. He could do a great deal of damage in her life. She had to be on her guard at all times.

"Okay. I want a Personal Pan Pizza with pepperoni and peppers," said Dallas to the woman, his elbows on the table, his chin propped on his hands. "And a Pepsi."

Both adults looked at him in astonishment.

"We have Coke," said the waitress.

"Oka-ay," said Dallas with a resigned sigh. "But that doesn't match the *P*."

"Excuse me for interrupting, but I have a correction to make," said his mother. "A small hamburger and cheese pizza, with milk to drink," she said.

Dallas tapped her on the shoulder and tilted his head winsomely when she looked back at him. "Lemonade?" he bargained.

West choked on a laugh and she nodded to the waitress. "Lemonade will be fine." She sighed heavily and closed her eyes.

"You want to split a large with everything?"

She opened her eyes to find West grinning at her. "No, I want a whole one of my own."

"Right." West finished giving their order and the waitress left.

She fixed her son with a stern eye. "You've been watching too much television."

"Mommy?" Dallas turned her face toward his. "Pepperoni-and-pepper pizza's on your own TV show with Abe. Remember?"

Lesley shook her head in defeat. "So it is." The restaurant was one of the new sponsors on the lunchtime show. She'd forgotten that was why she'd suggested it in the first place.

"I'd say you need to keep your strength up," West said, smiling. "Or should I say prowess, persistence, perseverance?"

Her mouth twitched—then she gave up and grinned back at him. "That's an understatement. It's his favorite game. He decides on a letter of the alphabet and drives people to distraction until they've thought of all the words they can remember that begin with that letter. Luckily he doesn't know too many letters yet."

"Yes, I do," Dallas corrected. "Newness taught me the alphabet song. 'ABCD, EFG, HIJK, LMNOP,'" he sang loudly. "*P* is for promises and plums."

"Remind me to fire her," growled Lesley, smiling to take the sting out of her words.

Dallas scrambled to his feet and looked over the back of the booth to an older woman who approached. "My mommy's gonna set you on fire."

Lesley started to turn, a horrified expression on her face. When she identified the woman, she relaxed. "Eunice, thank heavens."

"Is she, now?" said Eunice, reaching out to ruffle his hair. "Sounds pretty uncomfortable."

Dallas doubled over with giggles. "Newness, I was teasing."

"Do you really think she could find someone to replace me?"

"Not unless it was a someone who had never heard the alphabet song," said Lesley dryly. "Eunice I'd like for you to meet West Chadwick."

"Nothing gets past him, does it?" said West, rising to offer the older woman a seat. "Won't you join us for a pizza?"

"Thank you for asking, but I'm one of those weird people who don't care for pizza." Eunice returned his smile warmly.

Suddenly Lesley turned to her son. "Wait a minute. You said—"

"What?" asked Dallas.

"A minute ago you said 'pepper' and 'personal.'"

"And pepperoni pizza," added Dallas, not understanding the growing excitement in his mother's face.

"You can say 'R,' too—very clearly. When did this happen?"

Eunice smiled. "When the pizza parlor became one of your sponsors."

"So, TV does have its uses, I guess. Congratulations, Dallas."

"Thank you, Mommy," said the child, with satisfaction.

Eunice spoke up. "I just happened to be nearby and thought I'd see if Lesley was tired after the trip to the zoo."

West's smile worked wonders on Eunice, as Lesley could easily see. "I'm fine," Lesley protested. "Sit with us for a minute."

"Maybe for a minute."

West, who was still standing, let the older woman enter the booth first and sat on the bench seat beside her. She turned to him.

"Lesley has been up since three-thirty, you know."

He accepted that was supposed to make him feel guilty. He wasn't certain why. "So she told me."

"Dallas goes to bed at seven-thirty. Why don't I take him and his pizza home? Then the two of you can have yours in peace."

Silence greeted her words. West didn't know what to say. Did they not want him to spend time with Dallas? He looked at Lesley. Oddly, she was blushing. Had it not been for the soft color in her face he would have suspected they had planned this.

He wasn't aware that he had guessed right, but for the wrong reason.

He felt his anger grow and deliberately tamped it down. He wasn't going to make the mistake of jumping to conclusions. Not tonight. Lesley's invitation to join them had been a pleasant surprise. He'd wait and see what happened before he jumped in.

"He will start getting restless soon, I'm sure," said Lesley.

The waitress was back with their food. "Would you like to order, ma'am?" she asked Eunice.

"No, thank you."

But before the boy could move away, West made a suggestion. "Won't you have something to drink? Dallas is having lemonade."

Eunice shot him a sidewise glance. "Lemonade would be nice. Thank you."

Fifteen minutes later Eunice took Dallas home, the rest of his pizza in a doggie bag for lunch tomorrow.

West felt that he hadn't made a very good impression on the older woman. It was nothing overt, but he just had a feeling he'd not lived up to something she wanted him to be. He shrugged.

Maybe she was just reserving judgment. He couldn't object to that; in fact, he admired her for the quality. She had known him for less than a half hour.

West watched them leave, Dallas talking a mile a minute, before he turned to Lesley. "He's a fine boy. You've done a great job with him."

"I'm glad you think so," she said noncommittally, but she was pleased. She stirred her own lemonade with the straw and took a sip.

West froze for a moment, then watched, fascinated by the way her beautiful lips puckered around the straw. Her cheeks hollowed slightly as she sucked. He swallowed in an attempt to relieve his dry throat.

Suddenly a teenager squealed and laughed nearby, releasing him from her captivating spell. And bringing him back to reality.

He leaned an elbow on the table. "Last night you said that you hate liars, Lesley," he began, looking down to gather his thoughts. He raised his eyes to hers.

Lesley had to struggle to control her expression. She had suddenly, and quite unexpectedly, realized that his eyes were exactly like Dallas's eyes when he was being his most earnest. There was a certain angle of his chin, and the shape of his mouth—

"I hate them, too," he went on. "I understand your anger. I hadn't been totally honest with you and I apologize. I don't have an excuse, except that as I told you, I wanted to know what kind of person you are without lawyers between us. I was at a loss when I got the letter and was more or less exploring my way. I screwed up, and again I'm sorry."

"I accept your apology," she answered with a small smile. "Just don't ever do it again."

He might as well lay all his cards on the table. "I'm glad you feel like that, because I want to be completely open from here on out." He took a deep breath and let it out. "Every boy needs a masculine influence in his life. I hope we can work out something, so I can get to know Dallas and see him on a regular basis."

Her mouth dropped open. "A regular basis? You can't be serious," she responded. "Are we to tell him that you're his daddy, too?"

"I hadn't gotten that far. But . . . eventually, maybe."

"Maybe?" Her outrage was clear, but unexpected after the smile. "Maybe! You obviously have not thought this through. 'Maybe' doesn't work with kids."

"Can't we take it a step at a time? See what happens."

"Not with children. They think in terms of black and white." She leaned back, folding her arms across her chest. "Here's a hypothetical for you, West. What if you tell him you are his father, and he asks why you don't live with us?" She blushed slightly. "What are you going to say?"

West hesitated. "I—"

"Next fall Dallas goes to preschool, where he will be exposed daily to kids and questions. He knows he's adopted," she interrupted. "I was advised to make that clear from the first. He isn't quite sure what 'adopted' means yet, but he knows. When the time comes it will take very careful explaining, even as it does now. Then you show up and want to be a regular part of his life." She spread her hands. "He's going to be bewildered and confused."

"So I'm supposed to forget he exists? Not a chance."

"Why have you never married?" She blurted the question before she thought.

"You're kidding! With the example I had?"

"Your reputation is well-known, West. You're a rich, successful, swinging bachelor. You'll come into his life for a while, then leave."

"Leave? Why should I leave? And you've no right to cast aspersions on my life-style. A career woman with your sort of ambition doesn't make the best sort of mother. I know from experience."

His bitter statement brought her racing thoughts to a screeching stop. His sarcasm was more revealing than he knew. She hadn't realized just how much he resented his own mother. "Was your mother gone a lot?" she asked.

Lesley's soft tone, as though she were talking to a child—as though she were talking to Dallas himself, for God's sake—fueled West's anger. Nobody was going to assume he was insecure or vulnerable. Especially not this woman.

He narrowed his gaze and clenched his back teeth to keep himself from saying something he could regret. He deliberately pitched his tone to a calmer, lower level. "I guess I am a bit of a throwback when it comes to working mothers," he admitted. "I survived."

But she wasn't buying that. "Obviously not without scars. There are mothers who have to work, West."

"If they have to work, it's a different matter. If they want a considerable career, they don't have to have children."

"You mean they shouldn't," she snapped. She caught hold of her temper.

West didn't answer.

There was a long and heavy silence between them. At last she broke it. "You've given me a lot to think about, but I'll have to let you know." She gathered up her purse and sun hat.

"Don't wait too long."

"That sounds like a threat."

"Not a threat, a promise. Come on, I'll see you to your car." He reached for his wallet.

"No, thanks. I can make it on my own," she answered over her shoulder as she walked rapidly toward the door.

"Lesley," he called to her back. By the time he figured the tip and got outside, she was gone.

Chapter 5

"Do you want one of us to go with you?" Abe asked.

"Or both of us?" added Blanche, standing by his side. They had approached Lesley as she stood waiting for an elevator.

Lesley laid a hand on their shoulders. Her voice was husky with affection for these two terrific people. "Thanks, both of you. You're the best friends I could ever imagine having," she said, thinking how very true the idea was. She'd had many friends before, but because of her background she was wary of letting people become too close. She had never been as near to anyone as she was to them.

Abe and Blanche were like Lesley's extended family. When she had adopted Dallas, she had still been the station's consumer reporter. The job had been less exacting; except for her on-air time three times a week, she'd been able to do her research when it was convenient for her, and much of her writing at home. They'd been with her all the way.

And they were the only ones besides Eunice who knew that, with this new, more demanding job and unpleasant hours, she worried that she wasn't giving Dallas the time he needed. They saw her guilt. They knew all her doubts.

And, like Eunice, they had dismissed her guilty feelings.

"You're a lot better mother than I am," Blanche had once said. Blanche, divorced for ten years, had one teenaged son. Buddy was an acknowledged nerd. However, she amended, he was a nerd with a sense of humor.

But Lesley and Blanche both depended on Abe, who was engaged but not yet married, as a sounding board to give them advice about male children. He was the eldest of four boys, and his divorced mother had worked full-time, so he'd taken on responsibility at a young age.

The elevator doors opened and Abe put out a hand to keep them from closing again. "You're sure?"

Lesley nodded. "For now I don't think it's necessary. I'll simply explain the situation and find out what Mr. Hammond advises."

She was on her way to see the lawyer who had been highly recommended to her by the station's owner, Caroline Chandler, as a big gun. She had with her the file containing all the papers relating to Dallas's adoption. Although a woman from the legal department at the station had looked over the papers and pronounced them standard, both she and Caroline agreed with Blanche and Abe.

Though Caroline refused to believe that West Chadwick, whom she knew well, would cause Lesley trouble, she agreed that her employee needed her own lawyer, just in case.

"I can pretty much imagine what any lawyer's reaction is going to be," Blanche said ironically as Lesley stepped into the car.

"I'll tell you all about it in the morning," she promised. She smiled and waved goodbye, and the elevator doors closed between them. When she was alone, she let herself relax against the wall. She probably could have used the moral support of her friends, but she was determined to handle this herself for as long as possible.

Later, if things got hairy, she might need more than they were expecting to give.

Bill Hammond was a fortyish, overworked lawyer with a distinguished family practice, which meant he did everything from divorces and real estate to wills and adoptions. According to Caroline, he did them all very well.

Lesley liked his easy manner and his warm welcome from the first. His secretary had served them coffee and they had chatted for a moment. Now, as she sat across his desk from him, beginning her explanation, her confidence and trust were established by the gesture of hospitality and his quiet attention.

His eyes, distorted by thick glasses, never left her face, but he didn't hurry her as she told her story.

When she had finished, he took off the glasses and rubbed at his eyes before putting the glasses back on. "You say you saw this letter?"

"I saw a copy, but I recognized Valerie's—the mother's—handwriting. And though I hate to admit it, the man's physical resemblance to my son is striking," she added, West's image clear in her mind. "Their eyes are the same color and shape, their mouths are almost identical, and even some of the mannerisms—'' She broke off, shaking her head. ''His hair is darker blond, almost brown, but there are sun streaks across the crown. Dallas's hair turns lighter under the summer sun.''

She'd had ample time Friday night at the pizza parlor to observe and compare them. The similarities were remarkable, almost eerie. She had never been able to see more than a hint, a fleeting glimpse, of Valerie in her child; now she understood why. The potency of West's genes clearly prevailed over Valerie's.

Until now, she had refused to let herself think about the future more than she could absolutely help it. It would be pointless to worry until she spoke to a professional.

She had told her story to Eunice after she returned from the pizza parlor. The older woman had listened thoughtfully and agreed wholeheartedly that a lawyer should be the first priority.

Lesley had spent the remainder of the weekend, what there was of it, with Dallas, rarely letting him out of her sight. Eunice seemed to sense her need. She joined them when they went to the park, but Lesley and her son laughed at a show at the Center for Puppetry Arts alone together.

Dallas seemed a bit puzzled by his mother's enthusiastic energy, but he wasn't the type to look a gift horse in the mouth. He had enjoyed all the attention and would probably be spoiled rotten for poor Eunice by tonight when she resumed her schedule.

Lesley paused in the middle of her story, remembering, and Mr. Hammond watched her for a minute. He swiveled his chair in a short arc and back. He rested his elbows on the armrests, staring at her across his desk.

"I hate to tell you, Lesley, but if Mr. Chadwick demands DNA tests and they prove out, the man has a valid point. You're an intelligent woman. I'm sure you knew that."

"Yes," Lesley answered.

"It won't matter to the courts that Valerie lied to all concerned—at least, it hasn't mattered to them so far. Myself? I think the mothers who attest to a lie should be prosecuted for perjury."

"The poor woman is dead."

"You're more generous to her memory than I would be. She has left you in an untenable situation." He leaned forward, reaching for a pencil. "In any event I'm not sure that you should fight this. It will cost a great deal of money. And a win would be a miracle."

She lowered her head. "I understand. But Dallas is my son. I could never give him up without a fight, not if I have to work the rest of my life to pay for it."

"Do you want to sue the agency?"

"It isn't the agency's fault that Valerie lied."

He shook his head.

Before he could say more, she went on, "I investigated that agency thoroughly when I did the consumer story on them." Her voice broke; she clasped her hands in her lap and willed away the nerves.

"Look, Mr. Hammond, I'm not about to sue. I'll sign a release, a waiver—anything. Just help me. Tell me what to do. Last night, when he said he wanted regular visits..." Her dark-blue eyes sparked anger and frustration.

"I don't know anything about this man. He could be all kinds of horrible things...." One hand waved the air and she spit out her doubts one by one like bad-tasting bullets. "He could have the values of a slug, for all I know. He doesn't get along with his family. What kinds of people does he associate with? What would he teach Dallas? And with his bachelor life-style, is he competent to care for a child?"

Bill's eyes widened at her volatility. "West Chadwick? I doubt that any of your apprehension would apply to him," he said with a trace of irony. "Except maybe for the last concern. But he certainly can afford to hire anyone he needs, who is competent."

"Yes, his money and connections are issues I mustn't forget, must I?" she said sarcastically.

He withdrew slightly. "I hope you realize they are not issues that I would consider."

"Of course." She was quiet for a minute, hanging on to the anger for as long as possible. Then she let all the air out of her lungs. "I'm very scared, Mr. Hammond," she finally confided, her voice softened by her fear. "More scared than I've ever been in my life."

"My dear, of course you're scared." He rose from his desk and glanced out the window. Instead of sitting down again, he came around the desk and took the chair next to her. "I know West Chadwick slightly. By reputation, he's a top-notch lawyer and he does have a legitimate claim, no matter how much we would like to deny it. But he's also known to be a fair man. Maybe he'll back off of his own accord."

"I doubt that," she said. Against her will she reflected on the lovely, romantic evening they'd spent together before he'd dropped his bombshell. The evening that had been a lie.

"But if I'm lucky he'll find someone to really romance, and lose interest in me and Dallas." She frowned. Then she fixed the lawyer with her wide eyes. "But the question is, will you help me?"

"I'll help you," he said after a pause. "If you will listen to me carefully."

"Okay." She smiled, relieved for the first time since she'd entered the office. "Anything. Just tell me what to do."

He leaned an elbow on the arm of the chair and thought for a minute. "To start with, Lesley, I think you know what you have to do. You must reach some kind of agreement with this man. I can do it as your representative, but such a move would make your relationship officially adversarial. I don't think that is what you want. First, it would be better for you to try again.

"You may have to let him spend time with the child. With you present initially. Maybe later, if *and* after you are reassured about him, you may let him have the child alone."

"Right now I feel no compunction to do that," she said stubbornly. "He lied to me."

He nodded. "I can understand, but if you want me to represent you, you're going to have to try to forget the lie. You say you know his parents?"

"I interviewed them when they retired."

"And West seems to feel some bitterness toward his mother?"

"He respects her accomplishments," Lesley mused. "But I get the impression that, as far as he's concerned, she has sacrificed their chances for a close relationship in order to have a successful career," she added. She was sorry he hadn't had a good relationship with his parents, but it had nothing to do with her.

"And your high-profile career is a potential conflict," he reminded her. "Well, what you *don't* want to do is get into another argument with him. In fact, you may have to grit your teeth and make the first move."

"What! Me? Why should I..." Her voice trailed off as he waggled his brows at her.

"This is very important. You must demonstrate clearly your willingness to cooperate with the natural father of your child. Then, if you ever do have to go to court, the judge will have no reason not to look kindly on your petition."

"Damn. This just isn't fair. I'm supposed to just turn my child into a wishbone? To be pulled this way and that?"

"For now, it's your responsibility. Maybe someday the judges will come to their senses and see what they're doing to these children."

Lesley picked up her purse and got quickly to her feet. She gazed at the lawyer, who had also risen, and nodded firmly. "I'll do anything I have to do to have this resolved. Even make the first move."

On the way to West's office Lesley allowed her thoughts to wander back to the first days of Dallas's life.

Despite her instincts, she understood West's feelings about his mother. Despite her determination, her own doubts resurfaced.

One of the drawbacks to a successful career in journalism or in many other fields was often the lack of a stable and happy marriage. Though she knew she wanted a husband someday—if she ever found the right man—she was resigned to waiting until she was established in her career. That could be well past the age when she would want to have a child herself.

Valerie had suggested Lesley adopt her baby as soon as it was born. Now she couldn't imagine life without

Dallas. He might as well have come from her own womb. She would do anything to keep him.

Anything.

"Let me get this straight," West said a short while later. "You are inviting me to spend the day at Lake Lanier with you and Dallas."

"That's right," answered Lesley, ignoring his skepticism. "It will give us a chance to talk, and you can spend time with Dallas."

She had come to his office unannounced. The reception room was crowded. Betsy had given her a hard time for having no appointment, but the younger woman was nothing compared with Mrs. Riddock, West's secretary. *She* had given Lesley the third degree, even after Lesley had guaranteed she would take only five minutes.

"Please see that you do. He has to be in court this afternoon," said Mrs. Riddock.

At last, Lesley was sitting in his office. He'd taken the chair beside her rather than the one behind his desk. He wore a business suit and a dark, muted tie. The office setting and the somber clothes made him much more formidable.

But Lesley was determined to go through with this in as casual a manner as possible. "Tomorrow is Saturday. We can take a picnic to the beach area. Dallas loves to swim." She examined her nails with a show of indifference. "Of course, if you have other plans..."

"Yes," West answered quickly. "I mean, no, I don't have plans. I'd like to go. But why the turnaround? Both times we've been together I've managed to...upset you," he said. He let a small smile escape, turning up one side of his mouth. "In fact, you're usually mad as hell."

The understatement of the year, thought Lesley. "I told you I would think about your request. You were the one who was angry."

She watched from the corner of her eye. He wasn't going to lose his temper, but he was suspicious; it was there in every tense muscle of his body, the spasm of his jaw, in the way his eyes narrowed as he looked for a sign of dissimulation.

Feeling like the world's greatest hypocrite, she gave him her most sincere look. "I've decided that you and Dallas should get to know each other."

"So you're going to acknowledge that I'm his father?" he asked, still guarded.

"I didn't say that." She bristled, then calmed herself. "There would have to be tests. If Valerie lied about the father being dead, she could have lied about other things, as well."

"I see." He was quiet. When he spoke again, his tone was friendly. "Tomorrow is supposed to be a beautiful day. I'd like to go to the lake with you. What time shall I pick you up?"

"I'll pick you up. I think we should take my car. Spending a day out with a child calls for all sorts of paraphernalia."

"And my car is too small. I can see that." He nodded, but his inclination was to find an alternative. He wasn't a man who was accustomed to being called for.

"Would it be easier for me to meet you at your house?"

She didn't want to be obligated to ask him inside, before or after the trip. "No," she said, omitting clarification. "We usually wear our bathing suits under our clothes. I'm not sure whether there are changing cabanas or not."

"Okay," he said when it was clear she wouldn't explain. "May I bring something?"

She shook her head. "Eunice is preparing our lunch. She always makes too much."

He left her side and went to his desk drawer. "Here's a card with my home address. Do you know the area?"

"Yes," she said, examining the card. "I think so. Do I have to go through a gate?"

"I'll leave your name with the guard." He gave her directions, also, and agreed to be ready by eight the next morning.

The sky was a clear, bright blue once they left the city behind. West smiled and watched Dallas as he chattered to himself while he worked on a puzzle in the back seat. He was surrounded by toys—floating toys, a sand bucket and a shovel; and boats—sailboats, plastic cruisers, miniature wooden rowboats and a long, flexible, foam-rubber thing called a noodle.

Lesley looked terrific in white shorts and an aqua-marine camp shirt. Her legs were as long and beautiful, as West had known they'd be. But, except for a few platitudes about the weather and short answers to any subject he brought up, she was quiet. And the dark glasses she wore hid her expressive eyes from him.

West found himself in an unfamiliar situation and it was far from comfortable. He wasn't sure how to talk to Dallas, who was engrossed in his wooden puzzle.

Thank God and Eisenhower for interstate highways. It shouldn't take too much longer to reach the beach area of the lake.

Taking this trip with them may have been a big mistake. If she was tense with him, the child was certain to pick up on it—according to Alexandra.

He'd called his partner's wife last night, asking for child-care advice. When he'd admitted that he knew absolutely nothing about children, she'd roared with laughter.

"Do you mean you want me to tell you everything I've learned over sixteen years?" she'd asked when she could talk again.

"Well, not everything. But if you can give me some tips I'd appreciate it. I know David didn't exactly like me when we first met."

David was Alexandra's son, now Luke's stepson.

"It wasn't that he didn't like you. He just didn't like you for me."

"Why?"

There was a pause. "Are you sure you want to hear this?"

"I'm sure."

"Well, he had the impression that you were a playboy, who wasn't serious...."

West started to smile, when her next words wiped the smile from his face.

" 'Slick' was the word I think he used."

"Slick? God, that makes me sound like a hustling con artist."

"He was only fourteen at the time," she offered sympathetically. "He likes you now."

"Thanks," he said dryly. "That's a great comfort. Maybe I should ask David for advice."

He hung his elbow out the open car window and smiled, remembering Alexandra's renewed laughter.

"Why are you smiling?" asked Lesley.

It was the first time she had initiated a conversation and it made him hopeful. "I was thinking about my partner's stepson, David. He's a neat kid."

"Do they have children of their own?" she asked stiffly.

"David *is* Luke's son, though he's kept his late-father's name."

Just as Dallas is mine, Lesley wanted to claim solidly. But she held her tongue, remembering Mr. Hammond's instructions. She would say nice things, or she wouldn't speak at all.

"He was fourteen, and his mother was a widow. We were living in the same building when she and Luke met and married."

Now that they were talking, he didn't seem to want to stop. "You've seen the condos. All the buildings are the same shape. The large unit in the middle with three bedrooms belonged to Alexandra. Luke moved into the two-bedroom opposite mine while he was building a house."

"I see." She could hear herself sounding rather stilted. "What made you think of the boy?"

"I called his mother last night to see if she could remember anything about three-year-olds. I know very little about kids."

She masked her surprise that he had bothered to ask for guidance. "You were fine in the pizza parlor. Besides, you're speaking as though children are a different species entirely."

"As far as I'm concerned, they are. The pizza place was crowded. Today it's just the three of us. I've never had much contact with children," he confessed. "I thought she might be able to give me some advice on how to act around Dallas. So I wouldn't scare him."

She threw him a disbelieving glance. "You expected all that from one telephone conversation? Was she able to help?"

"She practically laughed me off the phone," he said, vexation in his voice.

That brought a smile to her lips at last. "Just be yourself," she advised.

"Dear God, no!"

That made *her* laugh.

The effect on West was electric. Once again she was the exciting woman with whom he'd had dinner last Friday. He didn't need that kind of distraction, but he was entranced.

"Okay, just follow my lead."

"Following you won't be a hardship at all."

The deep sensuality in his voice wiped the laughter from her face.

Lesley had planned this day to demonstrate to West Chadwick that she could be a good mother *and* handle a demanding career. But the sound of his voice was very sexy, very jolting to her peace of mind.

The surface of the lake was dotted with sails. Trails of water skiers made curved and sliding patterns in the wakes of the boats pulling them. The lakeside was lined with greenery—pines and oak trees, weeping willows near the shore, some magnolias with their large waxy leaves and, within the undergrowth, rhododendrons and mountain laurel, not yet in bloom. The man-made beach was crowded with families out to take advantage of the first really warm day of spring.

Dallas was out of the car and impatiently waiting for the grown-ups to unload. "Hurry, hurry. I want to swim." He had a swim ring around his waist—on top of his shorts and shirt. He plunked himself down beside the car and began to pull off his shoes.

"Dallas, get up," Lesley said as she lifted him under the arms and set him on his feet. "You know that parking lots are dangerous for little boys. And leave your shoes on until we get to the beach."

"Well, hurry, Mommy."

"You go on with him," West said. "I'll bring the ... paraphernalia."

"Thanks. I'll take an armful. The best spots are over this way. She grabbed a large, lime green tote bag with a purple animal painted on it and slung it over her shoulder. A folded quilt came next. And Dallas's hand.

West took the basket out of the car, surprised at the weight of the thing, and carried the toys, fitting the noodle under his arm, filling the pail with the shovel and one or two of the boats. The others he jammed into the waistband of his jeans.

Good Lord, he felt ridiculous.

West collapsed on the spread quilt in the shade beneath a willow tree. "I don't know how you do it. Where does he get his energy?" He was in pretty good shape, but Dallas could run rings around him.

They had splashed and played with boats in the shallows of the lake with Dallas. Then West and Lesley had each taken turns swimming while the other watched the boy shovel sand in the pail and dump it out again, build "castles" and bury his own legs in the sand.

When Lesley had first stripped off her shorts and shirt, West had had to make an effort to keep himself from staring at the redheaded vision revealed in a yellow bikini. The swimsuit was a conservative type, but it would have taken more than conservative to disguise her high, full breasts, the gentle curve of her waist flaring into a sweetly rounded bottom.

Now he was having the same trouble. Her damp skin was flawless, lightly tanned and smooth. She tossed a towel to West, dried Dallas's hair and tied a sarong-type thing around her middle.

The scrap of cloth concealed her almost to the ankle; he thought it was the most tantalizing piece of clothing he'd ever seen in his life.

She sank gracefully to the quilt. A beam of sunlight spilled across her back and one arm.

She opened the basket and began to pull out all kinds of food, some wrapped in foil, some in refrigerator containers. Paper plates followed, and napkins, plastic forks, knives and spoons.

"Lunch," said Dallas. "Newness fixed fried chicken," he told West.

West dragged his gaze away from her—it took an unexpected effort—and looked at the boy.

Be yourself, Lesley had said. He wasn't sure quite what that meant, but Alex had warned him not to talk down to the child. So far it seemed to have worked. Though Dallas didn't yet consider West his best friend, the child had not cringed from him.

"Is Newness a good cook?" he asked, smiling confidently at the boy. "I'm a connoisseur of fried chicken."

Dallas frowned. "A con-sewer? What's that?"

West's confidence disappeared in a breath. He threw a glance at Lesley, a plea for help.

Lesley had to hide a smile. "A connoisseur is someone who has eaten a lot of fried chicken," she explained to her son, "and knows good from bad," she finished as she started to fill his plate."

"Oh," answered Dallas. He frowned, pondering her explanation.

She was relieved to have something to do with her hands. Ever since they'd arrived and West had stripped off his knit shirt and jeans, leaving him clad only in his brief swim trunks, her breath had been shallow in her lungs, her eyes drawn like a magnet to his body.

She'd known his shoulders were broad, but not that they would be so hard and muscular, that the skin across his back would be tanned and smooth or that his iron-forged chest would be lightly sprinkled with hair.

Often as they played with Dallas, her arm would brush his, his leg would touch hers. She had no idea if he was as affected by the sight and touch of her scantily clothed body as she was by the sight and touch of his. He was truly a superb example of the male species.

She didn't know just how grateful she was for her son's habit of chattering until he interrupted her reverie.

"Newness fixes chicken better than good. I love it," he informed West. But he watched carefully as his mother served his plate. "I don't want salad."

"Just a little."

"Okay, but no deviled eggs," he said more firmly. "I don't like those lumps she puts in them."

"Those are pickles, Dallas, not lumps. Do you want a pimento cheese sandwich?"

Each decision had to be painstakingly weighed. "A half." He turned to West once more. "There's chocolate cake for dessert," he warned. "So you don't want to eat so much con-sewer that you won't have room for it."

West grinned and leaned toward the child. "I always have room for chocolate cake," he confided in a conspiratorial whisper.

Dallas grinned back. "Me, too. But my mom always makes me eat other stuff first."

Lesley watched, mesmerized, as the two facing profiles, which were so alike, smiled at each other. Her heart thrummed. She wanted nothing so much as to grab her son and run.

But, of course, that would defeat the whole purpose of this impossible day.

She took out two more plates and handed one to West. "Help yourself."

"This looks good." Dallas was engrossed in his food, so West took the opportunity to thank Lesley. "You were very quick with an answer for the 'con-sewer.' Thanks for pulling me out of the hole. I wouldn't have known how to explain."

"You said you called your partner's wife. What else did she tell you?" she asked around a bite of chicken.

"In a nutshell, Alexandra said not to talk down to Dallas. Unfortunately, I talked too far up."

"No, you didn't. She gave you very good advice. How will he ever expand his vocabulary if you guard your tongue? It's always better to explain. Even if he may not understand completely, he'll remember the word next time."

"Why are you telling me this?"

She shrugged. "Because you cared enough to ask, I guess."

West felt his spirits soar. He'd done something right!

They were quiet as they continued eating. Dallas and West each had a piece of cake. When they'd finished the child's face was covered with icing. Lesley took a washcloth from a plastic bag.

"May I?" asked West.

Lesley looked at him in surprise. "Be my guest." She handed him the cloth.

Dallas himself wasn't so sure. He pulled back and turned his face to the side. "Do you know how to wash faces?" he asked.

"I'm probably not as good as your mommy, but I'd like to learn."

"Okay." He held his face up.

West's hand was a bit unsteady, but he managed to get all the chocolate on the cloth.

"What do you say, Dallas?" prompted Lesley.

"Thank you, Wes'. I'm going to have my nap now," he declared. He lay down on his side between the adults but closest to West, surprising the man, and closed his eyes.

Once more, West looked to Lesley for an explanation.

"When he's awake he goes like a freight train with no brakes. But when he's ready to sleep, he sleeps, no matter where he is."

She gazed down fondly at the child, whose breathing was already regular.

West smiled, too. He stretched out a hand and brushed the pale hair from Dallas's forehead. Dallas's eyes opened briefly but didn't quite focus; then they shut again.

Lesley was touched by the way West had behaved today. He hadn't tried to force himself on Dallas, but he'd been there—to answer questions, to give him a ride on his shoulders, to play with him.

West played as though he'd never played before, as though he didn't know how. Her empathy had surfaced more than once, and she found herself helping ease the way for the two of them to enjoy each other.

As a child, she, too, had been tentative in her attempts to play. She had turned to books. She wondered what West had used as a substitute.

With Dallas, he'd been slightly awkward and hamfisted at first, but Dallas, too, was patient with him. And as he became more comfortable, he seemed fascinated by the boy and even affectionate to a point.

Dallas didn't sleep for very long. They swam again, cavorted in the playground. West pushed him carefully in the swing.

All the while Lesley watched. She was torn. Dallas was delighted to have a man at his beck and call, and what made him happy usually made her happy.

West was trying.

She didn't know how she felt about that.

Chapter 6

"Shall I carry him?" asked West later that afternoon. Dallas had gone to sleep again, just as quickly as before.

"Please," Lesley answered with a small smile. West had loaded the car, and all that remained now was the quilt. And a dry beach towel in which to wrap the child. "This has been an exciting day for him. He's worn-out. I'm tired myself."

West lifted up the child gingerly; Lesley folded the towel around him, picked up the quilt and carried it over her arm. "Don't worry. He won't wake up until he's ready. And heaven help the person who tries to wake him before that."

She moved ahead, assuming they would follow.

West looked down at the sleeping child in his arms.

Suddenly he felt a surge of emotion such as he'd never known before, not even the first time he'd laid eyes on this child. The warm, comforting weight next to his heart—he didn't know how to relate to the sensation. Or to his own reaction. A lump had risen in his throat and seemed determined to stay there.

He was unable to take his eyes off the peaceful face of his son. Thick lashes lay against a healthy pink cheek; his lips were parted just a fraction, enough to let his sweet breath in and out; a fist rested under his chin. He was a magnificent child.

West could have stood there forever . . . just watching him sleep.

Lesley had nearly reached the car. "West?" she called back questioningly.

He finally breathed, but it took added effort to pull himself free of the spellbinding trance.

He walked slowly, unsure if he was being careful not to wake the sleeping child, or if he was simply prolonging this priceless moment.

When they reached the car, he reluctantly settled Dallas in his car seat.

Lesley leaned in to tuck the towel around Dallas's bare feet and legs. "Thanks. He's getting heavy for me to carry." Then she realized what she'd said. She didn't want to reveal any sign of weakness where her child was concerned.

She tried to shrug off her remark. "But you know what they say about picking up a calf every day until he's grown."

West looked up suddenly, to find his face only inches from Lesley's. He started to make some comment, but whatever he'd been about to say fled his mind. Their gazes met and held, their breaths suspended. Without thinking, he closed the minuscule gap and touched his lips to hers.

Lesley was perfectly still. She savored the warmth of his mouth. It was a soft, sweet kiss, intimate but tender, romantic, not at all like the simmering, sizzling awareness they had felt when their bodies brushed on the dance floor.

While the moment was not as electrifying, she felt a substance, a depth, to the kiss that stunned her. He was the one to pull back.

"Why did you do that?" she asked gently.

"I don't know," he answered honestly and equally softly. "Did it offend you?" He smiled and tucked a strand of her soft, silky hair behind her ear, away from her sun-kissed cheek. She smelled like sunshine and tanning lotion. His pulse accelerated.

"I don't know." She repeated his words, then she blinked. "But matters could become very complicated if we let something like that happen again."

He looked at her, nodded and withdrew his head from the car. "Right."

She checked the fastening of the seat belt around her sleeping child before she followed. When they were both settled in the front seat, she spoke again. "I didn't mean that it wasn't a very nice kiss, but—" Her voice was hoarse and her hands weren't steady as she fastened her own shoulder harness and inserted the key in the ignition.

"I know what you meant. It was just a kiss. There are too many obstacles between us to try to tear them down with sex."

That wasn't *exactly* what she had meant, but she let it slide. The motor caught. "Right."

West lay sprawled on his stomach, sheets twisted around the lower half of his naked body.

His alarm sounded—a loud, harsh shriek. He'd shopped for the most uncivilized-sounding timepiece available on the market.

He didn't awaken easily, and this contraption had nothing so courteous as a snooze signal—it screamed at you to get your lazy self out of bed; you have things to do. He groaned and rolled over, slapping the button to turn the thing off.

He lay on his back for a minute, trying to gather his scattered thoughts. It was Sunday. Why had he set the alarm?

He stacked his hands beneath his head and looked at the ceiling, trying to recall. Then he groaned again. Mother's birthday.

He had been summoned for lunch and invited to a party at the club tonight. He'd accepted the lunch and declined the party. He knew what his parents' parties were like. Lots of Dom Pérignon and imported beluga. And far too many people he—or they—barely knew.

Now, if he were spending another day with another mother... he smiled at the memory of yesterday. Dallas had understated Eunice's touch. She had outdone herself with the chicken. And everything else about the day had been perfection.

He'd been suspicious when Lesley issued the invitation. He was a lawyer, after all. What did she have to gain? he asked himself. Money? No. Goodwill? That made him stop and think. He shook his head.

But after his suspicions abated, he had really enjoyed himself. Lesley was easy to talk to. He'd learned more about the circumstances surrounding Dallas's adoption, her apprehension, reservations and eventually her certainty that this was the right thing for her to do.

As a woman she was a delight to be with, not to mention very easy on the eyes. She was warm, generous, with a foxy sense of humor.

She was smart, could talk about anything, and when she played, she played all out. He smiled again, remembering the impromptu diving contest they had held for Dallas's amusement. She had won, of course; Dallas had been the referee; and every time he looked dubious about a decision she gave her son a mock pout.

West had particularly enjoyed the pout. Her bottom lip was full and moist when she presented it and her brows crinkled pitifully. He wouldn't have been able to resist, either.

West's smile faded. What the hell was the matter with him? He was supposed to be focusing on Dallas, not Lesley. Dallas was the important issue between them.

But he couldn't forget the promise, then the taste, of those lips; they were so sweet, so soft and yielding.

Maybe the kiss had been a mistake. Nevertheless, he couldn't regret that it had happened.

A random thought crept into his mind, a half-formed notion that they possibly might have a relationship of a sort. He firmly pushed the thought aside, along with the covers, and got to his feet.

He stretched, his arms over his head, and yawned. The exercise yesterday had forced him to take note of unused energy, and muscles that hadn't been tested for a long time. He needed to get back into a regular exercise routine. He dropped his arms and headed for the shower.

He stopped by an upscale shopping mall before heading for his parents' house. He went to a tennis shop his mother frequented and bought the newest tennis racket, one made of a lightweight alloy supposedly as strong as steel. The salesclerk, who was very familiar with Christine Chadwick, assured him that his mother did not have this racket.

While he waited for the gift to be wrapped, he wandered back out into the mall. Finally he reached what he realized what had been his destination all along—F. A. O. Schwarz toy store.

He wanted to buy a gift for his son. The first gift he would ever give Dallas suddenly seemed very important. He wondered for a brief moment about Lesley's reaction, then dismissed any misgivings. Surely she would understand how meaningful this would be to him.

When he came out forty-five minutes later, he was eighty-five-hundred dollars poorer. And he felt like a kid himself. The only thing he carried was one shopping bag.

He might have overdone it, he thought fleetingly, but what the hell? He'd had a ball. He did make one concession to easing his way into his son's affections. He'd called Alexandra for more advice; he told her about his purchases. After she'd gotten her breath back, she'd advised that he pick out one toy for Dallas to have now—she suggested the dump truck—and have the rest delivered to his condo. That way he wouldn't overwhelm the child or antagonize the mother.

He'd agreed and thanked her. But, after hanging up, he realized that he didn't have room in his condo, so he had arranged to have it all delivered to Luke and Alex's place, instead. They had plenty of room in their big house on the river.

He made his duty visit to his mother and father, had a gourmet luncheon served by a very proper butler and a new maid. His mother thanked him nicely, even enthusiastically, for the racket. She tilted her cheek up for a birthday kiss.

As quickly as he could get away he headed for Lesley's house.

No one was at home.

West could never remember having felt such frustration in his life. He sat on the front step and looked out over the lawn as he waited for a long, lonely hour.

Why not? He had nowhere else to go.

The house was beginning to grow on him, he noted about halfway through the hour. He lingered longer, while he composed a note to leave with the shopping bag.

Still no one arrived before he finally gave up and went home. But he had barely gotten in the door when the telephone started ringing. He grabbed it. "Hello?"

"Wes', this is Dallas MacDonald."

Dallas Chadwick, he amended silently. "Hello, Dallas. How are you?"

"Fine." He heard a whisper in the background and the child went on, "I've called you to say thank-you for the dum' truck." More whispering. "I needed one to play with in my sandbox. Did you know?"

West grinned. Dallas and Lesley had obviously rehearsed this, but the boy still relied upon his mother's prompting. "No, I didn't, but I'm glad I got something you needed."

"It's not my birthday," Dallas said hesitantly. "Can I keep it anyway?"

"Yes, you can. It's a thank-you present for letting me come to the lake yesterday with you and your mother."

"Do I have to let her have half?" He really sounded distressed.

West clamped his teeth over his lips to keep from laughing, but he didn't have a clue how to answer. "I guess you should ask her, but I doubt if she needs it as much as you do," he said at last.

Dallas's next words came over the line as a murmur that West had to strain to hear. "Wes', would you ask her for me?"

His heart swelled to double its normal size. "Sure. May I speak with her, please, Dallas?"

"Hello, West. I'm sorry we missed your visit."

The tone was that of the television personality, not the fun-loving woman of yesterday.

He did some fast thinking. "I hope you don't mind about the gift. I was buying my mother's birthday present today and saw the truck while I was in the mall. I probably should have checked with you first."

"It's all right, I guess," she answered, relenting somewhat.

He sensed her lack of enthusiasm through the wires that connected them and silently thanked Alexandra for her advice. He would send her roses tomorrow.

"It certainly is a fancy one," she said. "Dallas loves it."

"Is it too advanced for him? I would like for you to have seen it first, but the clerk assured me that a three-year-old would know how to run it. When I got to your house, I waited around for a few minutes—" a few minutes, hah! "—so I could show him how it worked. I'm sorry I missed you."

Lesley hid a smile. What had begun yesterday as an object lesson for a judge had ended as a truly enjoyable day. She wasn't certain that the kiss had been a good idea, but she wasn't going to worry about that. After all, it was only a kiss.

"He figured it out pretty quickly." She had an idea a thirty-three-year-old liked the big red truck, too. The thing had headlights and brake lights that functioned, a steering wheel that turned and an engine growl to rival a cement mixer. The dump part worked with the flip of a switch and the tires turned independently like a four-wheel-drive. "But, West, that truck must have cost a fortune," she said. "You know children are just as happy with inexpensive toys."

West felt himself turn white. She would really be outraged if she knew about the other toys. The electric train, the battery-driven car just large enough for Dallas to operate by himself and the room-size, polished maple fort with its ladders and slide, its cabin with a cutout window and a door on leather hinges. "It wasn't too bad," he said, hoping he sounded offhand.

Silence greeted his words. "Well, it's getting late," she said at last. "I guess I'd better go."

Late? Oh, yes. A smile spread across his face. "Eight o'clock bedtime tonight, right?"

She groaned. "Another week begins tomorrow. Dallas says thank-you. Or he would if he wasn't so busy with the truck. Again, we're sorry we missed you."

"I'm sorry, too." His voice dropped an octave. "I would have liked to see you again. I'll call you soon."

"I'd like that," she admitted. "Goodbye."

West hung up. His hand stayed on the receiver for a minute as though to prolong the contact. The idea that she would be asleep before he finished supper made him grin for some reason.

Lesley stood with her hand lightly touching the receiver, reluctant to completely break off the contact with West. For some reason—she wasn't absolutely certain why—the plastic under her hand felt slightly warm.

* * *

The following afternoon West was seated in the conference room of his office, surrounded by opened law books and yellow legal pads.

Betsy knocked softly and, without waiting for an answer, stuck her head around the door. Can you see Will McCarty?''

West made one more note, then tossed the pencil aside. He leaned back in the chair.

Will was the detective he'd hired to find Dallas. Their business was over. What was the man doing here now? He nodded to the receptionist. "Sure. Show him in."

West had a lot of respect for McCarty—the firm used him often—and he didn't want to offend the man.

Will had once been a lawyer, too, one who had practiced the profession for a few years and hated it. He'd gone back to school, gotten another degree—criminal justice—and started his own, very discreet private-detective agency. It was a decisive plus that he had a legal background, and West and Luke had been known to wait for weeks for his assistance—until he was free—when a case had to be handled with kid gloves.

But West was up to his eyebrows in work. Whatever it was that had brought Will here today, West hoped they could get it over with quickly.

"'Afternoon, Will."

"'Afternoon, West."

The men shook hands. "Have a seat. Coffee?"

The detective nodded and West in turn nodded to Betsy. He tipped a mug sitting beside him. Empty. "Me, too, please," he said, handing it to her.

When coffee was served and Betsy had disappeared, closing the door behind her, Will settled back in a chair at right angles to West's. "I may be sticking my nose in where it isn't wanted, but a few of my contacts got back to me after I finished the, uh, personal work—"

West waved his hand aside. "Luke knows about the child and about Lesley MacDonald. I showed him Valerie's letter and told him I'd hired you personally."

Will nodded. He tapped the edge of a file folder on his open palm. "You know how I hate loose ends. I found out a few more things about Ms. MacDonald that you might or might not need. But I have a hunch you'll probably want them. There may be something suspicious, or at least slack, about the agency, too."

"Tell me what you know."

"The adoption was brokered, as you know. I looked into the agency and it seemed to be on the up-and-up. But I heard from a friend of a friend that some of the couples who adopted their babies from there were showing signs of strain. As though they were extremely worried about something.

"I haven't delved that deep, but I did find out that Lesley MacDonald has seen a lawyer. Guess who?"

West didn't have to think about the question. "Bill Hammond is the best."

Will nodded.

"Lesley went to see Bill Hammond?"

"Right after you showed her the letter."

"She told me she might do that. And she has every right to," West mused. He stroked his chin with a knuckle. "But I've talked to her since and thought she'd given up the idea."

"I just bet you've talked to her since," Will remarked.

"What do you mean?"

"She wanted information, too. She wanted to know what kind of person you are."

West held up a hand. "I don't want to know how you knew that."

"I'm smart and nosy, not unethical," said Will, offended. "I happened to visit the studio. The lady's voice is trained. When she told her friends about her appointment, the door wasn't closed all the way."

Again West told himself that she had every right, even a responsibility, to question his motives. But hell, he didn't like it, and he couldn't pretend he did. "What else?" His voice took on a hard edge.

"She said she was totally willing if they had to go to court."

At that West erupted. "I told her we could avoid a court case if we behaved like responsible adults." The pencil he'd picked up snapped in two; he threw the parts halfway across the table. "I began this search in order to get to know my son. I had no intention of going for custody. She knew that—I told her." Hadn't he?

Will nodded. "Perhaps you should be prepared now, however. I heard her say that Hammond advised her to make very nice to you if she wanted the judge on her side."

West's brows drew together. "What?" So that was why he'd been invited to the lake Saturday. He didn't like this one damned bit. And he'd had no idea anything could dishearten him so deeply.

Despite the legal instincts that told him to collect some ammunition of his own, he found he didn't want to believe the worst of Lesley. On the other hand, he felt a swell of vindication.

Lesley had been indignant that he'd checked up on her. She'd been furious after he'd showed her the letter, had ordered him out of her house. Guilty conscience?

"Perhaps I should be prepared," he said reluctantly. "Can you stay on this for a while longer, Will? See what else you can dig up."

He told himself he was doing this for his son. But was he? He had been captivated by Lesley on Saturday. To find out now that she was exploiting his feelings for Dallas—it bothered him more than he wanted to admit.

He hardened his jaw. "I haven't decided whether I'll use it, but if there's anything to discredit her I want to know about it."

"Sure. The agency is the most promising lead. I'll leave this file with you."

"Thanks." He didn't feel thankful; he felt despicable. But determined.

"See you in a few days."

Will left and West rubbed his face roughly with his hands.

The setting sun had worked its way through the partially opened blinds, painting white stripes across the carpeted floor. He raked a hand through his hair. He'd long ago shed his coat and tie and rolled back his sleeves. The stack of open books seemed like a mountain. The yellow pads were filled with his scribblings.

Luke came into the conference room. He raised his brows when he saw the mess. "I'm heading home. Unless you need some help."

West dropped his pencil and stretched his arms over his head. He sighed.

"I'm about to quit for the day, too. I'll run the Chalmers case by you tomorrow if you have time, to see what you think."

"Sure. I'll try to get in early. See you in the morning."

West waved and started to bring order out of the chaos on the table.

Luke had reached the door, when he turned back. "By the way, how did the date go last week?"

West's eyes were drawn to Will's file, which lay at the other end of the table. "Shaky. But we spent the day at the lake this past Saturday with Dallas." His expression lightened. "He's the most remarkable kid, Luke. I think he has my eyes and—"

Luke laughed. "Save that for tomorrow, too. I have the strangest feeling that you're about to pull out pictures."

West linked his fingers behind his neck. "I don't have any pictures."

"Thank God," Luke said heartily.

"Yet." West grinned.

West didn't open the detective's file until he had finished with dinner, cleaned up after himself and settled down in front of the television to catch the ten o'clock news.

He realized that he had put it off for as long as possible. No matter what was in there he didn't really want to read it. But he had to.

Some lawyers could twist even the most innocent facts into testimony that sounded very sleazy. He'd always considered himself an honorable man, ethical even in the gray areas of the law. But how would he feel if it meant losing all contact with his child?

He wasn't sure how far he would go, and the uncertainty both worried and appalled him. What was he? Where were all his high-flown ideas when it came down to his own predicament?

Yesterday when he had held the sleeping child in his arms, he'd experienced an instinctive feeling of deep affection for the boy. Almost like love. The emotion, unlike any he had ever known, had left him tasting vulnerability. He hated it.

He turned off the television and opened the file.

The few usable facts were not particularly damaging—a rebellious childhood, an old boyfriend who had been in trouble with the police, an accusation of harassment from a company she had exposed when she was the consumer reporter for the station. On the witness stand, in the hands of a heartless lawyer, she could be made to sound trashy and unprincipled. Maybe.

If he really wanted to take her to court, not only would the law be on his side, but, he told himself, he could be cold-blooded enough to use these facts against her. Hell, yes, he could if necessary.

He slammed the file shut and sat with his hand on top as he stared into the middle distance. For a long time his mind churned over the information and the fact that she had asked him to go to the lake only at the advice of her lawyer.

At last he stood up wearily and headed for bed.

But he could not sleep. What would happen if he lost the case? The chances were slim to none. But Dallas, when he was old enough, could read about the angry confrontation between his mother and father.

What would such knowledge do to a child? Or to Lesley?

Chapter 7

Lesley was in the tub when the telephone rang. She ignored it as she lazily soaped one leg. She was tired tonight.

Two days ago, Monday had been like all Mondays, which the crew had long ago voted to abolish. But today, Wednesday, had been worse. During the noon program, Abe had been conducting a long-distance interview with a reclusive writer.

First they'd lost the video, but retained the audio portion. They filled the screen with a still photo. That wasn't too bad. When the video was restored, they all breathed a sigh of relief.

Until the audio began to break up.

Abe, who was normally the easiest-going man in the world, almost lost it. She could see the frustration build in him.

A red light appeared on the closest camera. She smiled brightly and said, "Let's take a pause for the cause, while we attempt to solve these technical problems. We'll be back after this message from our sponsors."

And they went to commercial, luckily before Abe's colorful language could go out over the air. She chuckled; he rarely cursed and barely knew how, but he'd outdone himself today.

She finally rose, dripping, from the tub. She dried herself, rubbed in her favorite body lotion and slapped a powder puff in a few places. Her sleep shirt was halfway over her head, when abruptly, her movements stopped.

The telephone. What if it had been West? She hadn't heard from him since they'd talked on Sunday.

Wrapped in a bathrobe, she padded into the kitchen. "Who was that on the phone?" she asked mildly.

Eunice was loading the dishwasher. She dried her hands and picked up a slip of paper. "It was long distance. I took down the name and number," Eunice told her. "He said it was very important."

Lesley felt curiously let down but took the paper from Eunice. She frowned. "He wouldn't be calling me if he didn't think it was important," she confirmed, looking at Eunice. "What in the world could Mr. Hampton want?" she wondered aloud.

"He didn't say, just that he wanted you to call him back."

"Davis Hampton was my high-school principal," Lesley explained absently. "He believed in me when a lot of people didn't. He also helped me get my first scholarship. I haven't heard from him in years."

She turned to the phone, punched in the number and listened to the ring on the other end. Her brows were still furrowed in confusion.

When she hung up ten minutes later, she was pale with anger.

"The bastard," she growled. "The rotten bastard."

"Davis Hampton?" Eunice asked from the other side of the room, where she was wiping the counter.

"No, no, not him." Lesley's jaw was as hard as steel. "*Mr.* Westmoreland Chadwick."

The following afternoon, Thursday, Lesley summoned a smile, albeit a bland one, for the receptionist at the firm of Quinlan and Chadwick. One more day until the weekend. Not only was she unusually tired today, but she was also in the enemy camp, and she didn't plan to give an inch. "Hi, I'm—"

"Yes, Ms. MacDonald, I'm Betsy. We met last week."

"I called earlier for an appointment with Mr. Chadwick."

Betsy got to her feet. "And I'm to show you right in." The young woman crossed the reception area to a door and opened it. "Ms. MacDonald is here," she announced to the man behind the desk.

"Lesley, come in." West closed a large volume and rose with a welcoming smile that didn't quite reach his clouded eyes. He indicated a chair next to his own, to the side of his desk. Instead she took the one that put the width of the desk between them.

He knew from her expression that she was angry, though she tried valiantly to hide her hostility. He'd known when Betsy had told him Lesley had made an appointment, asking first how much he charged for an hour. He wasn't even sure about the acceptability of this meeting. She had her own lawyer.

Moreover, if she wanted to talk to him, she could simply have called. She had no need for a formal appointment.

He watched as she settled herself with those little feminine gestures that were such a part of her. She smoothed her skirt, placed her purse neatly in her lap and crossed her hands casually on top.

He was annoyed with himself for noticing.

He was angry, as well; had been ever since he'd talked to Will. He sat down in his chair. "How's Dallas?" he asked.

"Dallas is fine. But this has nothing to do with him. I want you to know straight up front that I intend to pay for your time."

He raised a brow. "Really?"

"I came to demand that you call off the person or people who are following or investigating me. I am referring to the ones who are phoning my friends and asking inappropriate and irrelevant questions."

He was silent.

"I have worked very, very hard to reach a level of responsibility. Getting through school, finding a job, working my way up was not easy."

He acknowledged her statement with a nod.

"Unlike you, I didn't have anyone to pay my bills while I was in college or graduate school," she snapped. Her voice was rising. "My performance got me where I am. My good name is the only thing that will keep me there. A solid reputation for responsibility is everything to a journalist. Your people, with their inquiries, are planting seeds of doubt in the friends and business associates who mean the most to me."

His jaw jerked, then hardened. "What do you think? That you have a monopoly on reputation? A good name is everything to a lawyer, too."

She took a long breath in an attempt to calm herself. "I had a call last night from Columbus, from my high-school principal, for pity's sake. Mr. Hampton wanted to know if I was in trouble. I don't like his having to ask me that. This man was an important part of my life. He was the first one to teach me that I could be somebody.

"He said that someone had been asking questions of anyone in Columbus who would talk about me. He wanted to know what I had gotten myself involved in."

West's eyes narrowed, he leaned forward and spoke slowly. Though he was surprised that Will had let this happen, he still was grateful for the information the man had gathered.

"Let me ask *you* something, Lesley. When Valerie died, I received the shock of my life—by letter, no less. After I learned that you had adopted my son, did you expect me to just accept the situation without trying to find out about you? If the situations were reversed, wouldn't you want to know what kind of person *I* am?"

She didn't answer, but her chin lifted a fraction.

"I'd like an explanation for your own actions," he said. "Why did you invite me to go to the lake with you Saturday? The trip wasn't the spur-of-the-moment thing you led me to believe, was it? Didn't you think your status would be more defensible if you seemed to be friendly with Dallas's father?"

Lesley was stunned by his insight—or was it insight? Of course it wasn't; his snoops had been at work again. Suddenly she knew how a witness felt under cross-examination by this man—like cringing.

"And I also have some questions about this adoption agency you used."

She heard the sneer in his tone, but with the mention of the agency, she was on more solid ground. "I investigated the agency myself," she said, pointing her finger at her chest. "In *depth*. I have no doubts about their good standing. I hope your innuendos won't make people question their good reputation."

They were both leaning forward, half sitting, half standing. It was a good thing the desk was between them or they might have come to blows. "There are people who do have questions and doubts. Some of them are the adoptive parents themselves."

Suddenly the door opened.

Luke Quinlan stuck his head in. "Hey, guys, calm down. I can hear you all the way in my office."

"I'm sorry," said Lesley, embarrassed to her toes. She never lost her temper, much less shouted. But, as she looked at the tall, frowning stranger, she realized that she and West had done their share of both during the past few minutes. She let out a breath and settled back in her chair. "Please forgive me. I'm Lesley Mac-Donald. You must be—?"

West spoke before Luke could answer. "My partner, Luke Quinlan. Sorry, Luke. We'll keep it down."

"Thank you." Luke withdrew, pulling the door closed behind him. A ponderous silence stretched between Lesley and West.

Finally Lesley said evenly, "I don't believe any of your accusations about the agency. You're just trying to change the subject, which is your investigation of me.

"I am paying for your time. And I want to spend that time on the subject. I demand that you call off your snoops immediately."

"Private detective, singular, not a snoop. And you can have the time free if you'll explain about Saturday. I thought—" He broke off, afraid he'd say something he'd regret.

"I don't *want* it free." She reached into her purse and withdrew a check already made out and signed. She tossed it across the desk toward him. Her jerky movement caused a breeze that picked up the check and dropped it on the floor.

West retrieved it and laid it on the edge of the desk directly in front of her. "I'm not going to take your money."

She ignored the piece of paper. "So? What's your answer?"

West ran a tired hand over his face. "One private detective," he repeated. "We've used him many times and he is known for his discretion."

"Plainly, he screwed up this time."

"Lesley, the investigation is over anyway. All you had to do was ask. I would have told you."

That took the wind out of her sails. "I'm glad to hear that," she snapped. "What do you plan to do with the information you've gathered?"

He shrugged. "I don't know. File it, I guess."

"To hold over my head? Do you plan to go to court?" She shook her head violently. She couldn't believe she'd blurted out that question. "Forget I asked that."

"I certainly will. You said this meeting had nothing to do with Dallas. I took you at your word, and you have your own lawyer to advise you. But I'm not a blackmailer, Lesley."

She felt heat rise in her cheeks. "What about the agency?" she asked, to get back on track.

"I still plan to look into them further." He didn't tell her why.

"I've already gone through that business with a fine-tooth comb. I investigated more than one private agency, you know. There are some bad apples in this business. The agency I used is not one of them. In fact, it was one of the top three in the city." Her jaw took on a determined tilt. "These people do a lot of good. There's nothing wrong with their operation."

"How long has it been since your investigation? Three years? More than three years, isn't it? Have you had contact with them since?"

She longed to be able to slap that sneer off his handsome face. "No. But I have no reason to believe anything's changed—"

"Maybe you should find a reason," he interrupted.

"Consumer reporting isn't my job anymore." She rose, tucking her purse under her arm, ready to get out of there. More than ready.

The argument had left her feeling short of breath, claustrophobic. West was such a presence that he seemed to dominate the room. And her.

Her heart began to thud. She couldn't deny that she had begun to have feelings for him. She wouldn't deny her motive for the trip to the lake Saturday, but it had turned into something more than she'd expected. Much, much more, she thought, remembering the kindness he'd shown Dallas—and the kiss.

Coming to see him had been a mistake, but what choice had she had? "Goodbye, West."

"Take your check with you."

"No. I made the appointment. I'll pay for it."

He muttered something under his breath and came around the desk. He picked up the check, deliberately holding her gaze as he tore it into little pieces. Then he reached for her hand. He slapped the pieces into her palm.

Her jaw slack with surprise, she reacted automatically, closing her fingers. Some pieces stayed within her grip; some fluttered to the floor.

The heat of his hand beneath hers held them both motionless for a second. Then he dropped his hold as if he'd been burned.

West pondered his alternatives for twenty-four hours, almost to the exclusion of everything else. He'd talked to Luke about the scene in his office. He'd described the details of Lesley's difficult upbringing and her fight to become a successful journalist.

"So you're not going to try to gain custody?" Luke asked Friday afternoon.

"I don't think I ever really intended to go that far," West admitted. He rose from his desk, slid his hands into the pockets of his jeans and went to the window. He adjusted the blinds and stared out.

When he spoke again, his voice was emotionless. "Not unless there was a major problem. And there isn't. Lesley is a terrific mother."

"I do want to see Dallas on a regular basis." He turned his bleak gaze to Luke. "She's so angry I doubt that she'll listen to me."

"And Lesley?" Luke inquired quietly. "Would you like to see her on a regular basis, too? She's quite a woman."

West heaved a sigh. "That she is, and yes, I would like to see her again. But, I'm afraid she isn't feeling very charitable toward me right now. Hell, she hates my guts."

Luke nodded thoughtfully. "And getting involved with her would certainly complicate any relationship with your son."

"Luke, I'd like to legitimize Dallas." Legitimization was a fairly simple process. All he had to do was swear that the child was his.

"What would Lesley have to say about that? He's already legitimate, you know. He's been adopted."

"Yeah. But not as far as his father is concerned." West crossed one foot at the other knee. "Hell, Lesley would probably tell me to take a hike. But he's my son. I want to have a genuine role in his life."

"The legality of the adoption may be your only route," said Luke, watching him carefully.

"I won't take him away from the only mother he's ever known."

Luke grinned widely. His expression was clearly one of relief. "I'm very glad to hear you say that, pal. Cases like this are a cruel part of the law. Nobody wins—certainly not the child. Now, what about this agency?"

"Lesley swears they're on the up-and-up. But if she could read what Will has dug—"

Luke interrupted him. "Why can't she?"

West, his jaw agape, stared at Luke. "Why indeed," he said softly after a moment. "Why not?"

Lesley had thought Friday would never end. After the debacle in West's office yesterday, she hadn't slept well, earning herself another questioning look from Roy as he applied concealer underneath her eyes. At least the programs went without a hitch.

Eunice was having dinner with an old friend, but she had prepared a casserole for Lesley to reheat and a congealed salad that was Dallas's favorite.

Dallas was in a good mood during dinner; they watched a Disney movie together—a rare treat for him to have his mother's undivided attention—and he went to bed with no complaints.

When Lesley was alone she poured herself a glass of burgundy and settled in the living room with a book, a mystery she'd been wanting to read. But the pages held no interest.

At last she laid the book aside and tucked her feet up under her while she sipped the rich wine. She sat there, staring ahead, for a long time and let her mind wander. When her thoughts landed on West or Dallas or what she was going to do about the quandary the two presented, she methodically set them aside.

She would have to reflect, to ponder what to do about both of them, but not now, not tonight. Tonight she was too tired, too wrung out, too susceptible to emotion. Maybe tomorrow she would be thinking more clearly.

In the meantime, she was ready for bed. She drained the last sip of wine from the glass and was on her way to the kitchen, when the doorbell rang.

She glanced at her watch. It wasn't as late as she'd thought. She detoured to the door and looked through the tiny glass bubble, to find West standing there.

Surprise was too mild a word to describe her reaction. She opened the door.

He held a large cardboard box labeled "Saltines" and he appeared as tired as she felt. His face was drawn, pale in the overhead porch light. His shirt looked as though it had never seen an iron and his jeans bagged at the knees. His running shoes had had better days.

She detected an unexpected increase in her pulse rate. "Hi," she said.

"Hi," he answered, his tone and expression noncommittal. "I've brought you the files. I decided you needed to see them for yourself."

"About the agency?" She'd finally admitted to herself yesterday that she was curious. She still believed in the agency, but her reporter's nose wouldn't let her ignore the hints he'd given.

"All of them. About you, too. I decided I didn't want them."

She was speechless. She stepped aside and he deposited the box on the floor.

He moved back to the threshold. "You can call if you have any questions."

"West . . ." she didn't know what to say.

Before she could come up with a response he'd gone.

He'd put the onus square on her shoulders, she realized the next morning when she began to go through the files. She skimmed over the ones pertaining to her own life and career.

She delved more deeply into the interviews the detective—his name, Will, was on the memos—had managed to get with some of the parents who had adopted children from the agency. Many of them were reluctant to speak. It was easy to see why.

Some of them had been informed that a mother had changed her mind, a father had decided he wanted custody, there had been a mix-up in the records—all the nightmares adoptive parents experienced. When asked about testifying they were all terrified and unwilling to go public. One or two of them explained that the problems had been worked out, which she took to mean that they had paid some money to someone.

"Mommy, are you going to read all day?" her son whined from the doorway to the hall. She had spent the better part of the morning on the living-room floor with files spread out around her.

She made herself smile, though the stories she was reading made her want to cry, instead. She could understand Dallas's frustration. With few exceptions, Saturday was his day, their day to spend together. "No, sweetheart, just a few minutes more."

He wandered off. She needed to go over these more carefully before she made a decision, but on the spur of the moment, she decided to call West and apologize. Clearly the agency—or someone who worked there—had some answering to do. She hoped it was the latter.

She rose from where she sat Indian-style on the floor and headed for the phone in her bedroom.

He answered.

"West, this is Lesley. I—" She broke off when she realized she had reached his answering machine. She waited impatiently for the tone.

"West, this is Lesley. I read the file and I hope you'll accept my apology for not believing you about the agency. You were right. Another investigation is definitely called for. If you'd like to have dinner with me tonight, we can talk about this some more."

She hung up the phone and called out to Dallas. "Hey, slugger. Want to toss the ball around for a while?"

"Yes, yes, Mommy. I'll get my cap."

"Lesley, telephone," Eunice called from the back patio.

"Oh, Mommy," Dallas complained.

They'd been playing only a short time. He came over and grabbed one of her legs, swinging back and forth. The Braves baseball cap, which was far too big, tilted sideways over one eye.

Love for him rushed through her like crashing rapids. "I'll be back in a minute, sweetheart."

"O-kay," he said mournfully.

Her guilt, the feelings she had confessed to her co-workers, kicked in. "Want an ice-cream cone?"

The sadness disappeared in an instant. He punched the air above his head with his small fist. "Yes!"

Too much television, she thought once more. "Yes, what?"

"Yes, please, ma'am."

Eunice held the door for them. Dallas reached it about ten steps before she did. "It's West," Eunice told her.

Dallas ran to the telephone and grabbed it before Lesley could reach his side.

"Hi, Wes'. It's Dallas. I'm going to have an ice-cream cone."

Lesley smiled as she listened.

She could tell that the older woman was dying to know what was going on. She certainly had not tried to hide her fury after the call from Davis Hampton. "I left a message on his machine," she said casually.

"I'll get the ice cream," Eunice said.

"Thanks." Lesley crossed the room.

Dallas handed the receiver to her. "If he asks for me, tell him I'm not here."

She looked at her son blankly and shook her head in confusion. Finally she raised the receiver to her ear. "Hi, West. Thanks for returning my call."

He was chuckling. "Did he say what I thought I heard him say?"

"I'm afraid so. Sometimes he doesn't get things quite right."

"Did I hear *you* right? Did you ask me to dinner?"

She felt heat climb her neck. "Yes. I've been going over the files about the agency. I'd like to talk to you about these reports." Her hand was damp and she gripped the receiver more tightly. After the emotional scene in his office he must be wondering if she was quite sane.

"The other files, I'd like to try to forget about for a while," she added quietly. "If you'll forget for a while about my motives for asking you to the lake."

There was a slight pause and she knew the wheels were turning in his head. "Okay. We can give it a shot. What time?"

"None of these reports have names attached, just initials," Lesley said. She had picked up the reports from the living-room floor and stacked them in their original order on the coffee table before the sofa.

"Will promised these people anonymity for now. If we decide we want to talk to them, he'll try to get their permission."

West had brought a chilled bottle of wine from a vineyard in the North Georgia Mountains. He'd been clearly dissatisfied that Dallas wasn't here. And slightly suspicious.

Now they sat an arm's length apart and sipped the dry, crisp wine, while West scanned through the notes she'd made about her investigation of the private adoption agency.

"Those notes are all from memory. I may have more information in the old files at the studio. But, then again, I may have nothing. The woman who took over from me might have disposed of them. I can ask."

West nodded. "I can see why you thought they were clean. Your investigation was very complete."

Quid pro quo, thought Lesley. "Thanks. And I can see that you would doubt me, after reading those." Lifting her wineglass, she indicated the files on the table.

"I intend to renew the investigation, or at least pass it on to my successor. But I want to be sure of what we have before I make any kind of accusation. And it worries me that the place doesn't seem to be making money. If the founders and the whole staff are involved . . ."

"Maybe they aren't. I've been thinking along the same lines. Only one or two people could be threatening the parents with blackmail."

"He's sure about that part of it? I can't help but wonder why I haven't been contacted. I would appear to be a perfect target if it is blackmail—single mother, high profile."

"He's sure. That's about the only thing these people would say to him. When we find out how the scam works, we'll know why they didn't approach you."

"Do you think your man—Will—would ask if I could talk to some of these couples?"

"We'll talk to them together."

She opened her mouth to protest. Then closed it again. This was no time to antagonize him anew.

But, like some kind of transcendental soothsayer, he knew exactly what she'd been about to say. "Lesley, I'm in this with you. Whether you like it or not Dallas is my son. What affects him affects me. You and I have many problems to resolve, but I hope you've accepted that one fact."

Silently, she sipped from her wineglass and eyed him sideways. He wore khakis, dock shoes and a blue dress shirt, open at the throat, sleeves rolled back. The hair above his open shirt collar and on his muscular forearms was a shade darker than his light-brown hair.

The tall lamp on the table beside him reflected off the sun streaks in the thick hair that brushed the back of his neck. That same lamp, fitted with a bright reading bulb, turned his azure eyes an even lighter blue. But she no longer thought of his eyes as icy. No, they held all the warmth of a Southern summer sky.

Dallas's eyes. "Yes, I've accepted that you are his father." She realized that with the admission, she was leaving herself vulnerable.

"Thank you for that," he said quietly.

He reached out, covered her right hand with his left. She felt the zing of electricity travel from his skin to hers, and tried to withdraw.

But her hand, though not restrained, was trapped.

She refused to meet his eyes lest her gaze be trapped, too. She looked, instead, at the clock on the mantel. "I didn't realize it had gotten so late. I imagine you're hungry. Dallas and Eunice will be home soon and I haven't even started dinner."

West lifted his hand, releasing her. Then she was sorry. She experienced a feeling of abandonment. Her hand felt chillingly empty. She curled her fingers into her palm.

"I'll help," he said.

The trace of huskiness in his voice pleased her. He'd been affected, also. The knowledge helped her regain her emotional balance. She smiled at him. "I have to admit that I'm not much of a cook. Eunice prepared everything. All I have to do is set the table and put stuff in the oven.''

He laughed, a deep, warm sound. When he got to his feet, he grabbed her hand again, using it to pull her up beside him. "God, I'm glad to hear that. You've been trying to convince me you're supermom and I was close to being a believer."

Lesley sipped a second glass of wine and stood beside the oven. The casserole was nearly done; just a tad browner on top and she would take it out. Wonderful scents of rosemary and thyme and chicken filled the room. The bread sat on the back of the stove in a napkin-lined basket, covered with a cloth to keep it warm.

West had insisted on making the salad while she set the table for four. He had chopped, torn and diced with an efficiency that surprised her.

"I've lived alone for years," he explained, setting the salad bowl on the table. "I had to learn a few things or I would have starved."

"I've lived alone for years, too. Haven't you ever heard of takeout?"

"As in take the casserole out of the oven before it gets dry," West suggested, returning to her side. He rested one hip against the countertop.

"You're the expert," she answered, setting aside her wineglass.

He caught his breath as she bent to remove the casserole from the oven. Her jeans stretched tight across her rounded bottom.

She had no idea of the effect on him.

Since he'd arrived, the atmosphere between them had been unsteady. She was trying as hard as he to keep the essence of the afternoon on level ground. But his attempts were forgotten as she straightened and placed the casserole on the stove.

He reached out, plucked the protective mitts from her hands, tossed them on the counter and pulled her between his long legs. She looked suddenly surprised, but she didn't protest.

The heat from the oven had flushed her face becomingly. He framed it with his hands, the way Dallas did when he wanted her full attention. "You know what I'm going to do." It wasn't a question.

She should push herself away. She placed her hands on his chest to do just that, but somehow they betrayed her. Instead she slipped her fingers between the buttons on his shirt until she reached bare, slightly rough skin. She felt heat building in her lower stomach, then moisture in her most intimate place. She felt as though she were awakening from a long, barren sleep.

"Yes," she whispered, drawing his gaze to her lips for a brief second. "Look at my eyes," she ordered softly.

He did. His gaze locked with hers.

She raised her arms to his shoulders, bringing her soft breasts into contact with his hard chest. "Am I complaining?"

West's arms instantly encircled her slim body; his forehead dropped to hers. "I knew you would feel like this in my arms." His mouth curled into a smile of release, of desire, of passion. "Or maybe I dreamed it." Then his mouth covered hers, with a hunger, a thirst, a craving that stunned him.

His hands dropped to her waist, then slid into the back pockets of her jeans. He fought the burning instinct that would have had her on the floor beneath him while he plunged into her over and over and over.

Instead he made himself move slowly as he brought her forward, until she was nestled between his legs, thigh to thigh, belly to belly. He shifted his hips slightly and spread his legs wider. He adjusted, brought her even closer until her heat almost encompassed him, as close as possible except for the clothes between them. They fitted precisely.

The sizzling desire that had been an undercurrent between them from the first, burst into flames.

"West," she murmured.

Her breathing grew shallow; her head fell back, exposing her long, beautiful neck to his hot mouth. As he ran kisses across her throat, he felt her racing pulse. His hands massaged her bottom, never letting up the pressure that molded her to him.

She shifted her upper torso against him, as though pleading for his touch elsewhere, and he almost lost it. He slid a hand up her back to the fastening of her bra. He slipped the hook; then his fingers found one warm, full breast, clasping her fullness in his big hand, squeezing just hard enough to stimulate a groan, pinching her nipple gently, drawing a gasp of pleasure from her.

Lesley knew she would be but a puddle on the floor had he not held her in his arms. But she wanted to feel him skin to skin. She pulled her fingers loose from where they had tangled in his hair and tore at the buttons of his shirt.

She had undone maybe three of the buttons, when he caught her by the wrists. "There's a damned car outside," he growled.

She could have cried buckets of tears. All the muscles that had tightened with passion and longing relaxed at once and she slumped in his arms.

"Hey, red. I need to get control of myself." His hands shook as he guided her to a chair and sat her down.

As he backed up, though, he kept his eyes fixed on hers. "You are one wickedly desirable woman, Lesley MacDonald," he told her in a low, dangerous voice. "Someday I'm going to have you, or die trying. And right now that seems a distinct possibility."

"But not very satisfying," she countered, her own voice trembling.

Dallas's high-pitched laughter reached her ears. She smoothed her hair back, refastened her bra and straightened her shirt. He adjusted himself with a look of painful regret and started to work on his buttons.

All the while their blue eyes, hers dark as midnight, his light and slightly stormy, remained locked.

Chapter 8

By the time the back door opened to admit Eunice and Dallas, West was filling the glasses with ice and Lesley had the pitcher of tea in her hand.

"Hi, how was the movie?" she asked cheerfully.

"It was taller than me," Dallas said with disdain as he crossed the room.

"It was over his head," Eunice translated absently. Her gaze moved from Lesley to West. She picked up the child and sat him on the counter; she washed and dried his hands. "I should have known. Just because a movie says Disney doesn't mean it's appropriate for a three-year-old," she added as she set him on his feet.

"I'm sure it didn't hurt him." Lesley smiled at her. "Your timing is perfect. I just took the casserole out of the oven. West made a salad."

"Does that mean I have to eat it?" demanded Dallas, still out of sorts.

He eyed his mother and West, evidently picking up the tension in the room. Surely he couldn't pick up the reason. "You wouldn't want West to have his feelings hurt, would you?" she asked.

Dallas came over and stood looking up at the man. "I'm a con-sewer of salad. It better be good."

West, who had still been breathing hard, let out a whoop. Lesley and Eunice laughed, too. "If it isn't, I'm sure you'll tell me," West said, grinning at his son.

The byplay diffused the apprehension, relieving him mightily. Without thinking, he reached down to lift the boy high into the air.

Eunice inhaled audibly.

West glanced at her, caught her frown and slowly lowered Dallas to his feet. "Lesley, do you want me to cut a lemon for the tea?" he said.

"Please. Bottom drawer," she answered, indicating the open refrigerator door. She, evidently, had missed her friend's displeasure.

West retrieved a lemon, found a dish and cut the fruit into wedges; then he joined the others at the table. He unfolded his napkin and plunged in. "Eunice, if your casserole is as good as your fried chicken, I'm your slave forever."

The older woman smiled, though the expression didn't quite reach her eyes. "Thank you, West. Coming from a 'con-sewer,' I consider that a real compliment."

"I told Newness about you being a con-sewer. She didn't know what it was, either. I 'splained."

The mood throughout the rest of the meal was moderately relaxed. If Lesley blushed occasionally when her gaze collided with West's, if he grew silent at the sight, neither Eunice nor Dallas seemed to notice or comment.

Dallas's attention was mostly directed at West. As their guest, he was someone new to talk to, and he always answered.

They finished the meal with a bread pudding topped with rich caramel sauce. West had also brought a package of Jamaican Blue Mountain coffee, which they drank with the sweet.

West and Lesley offered to help with the dishes, but Eunice declined. She sent the three of them into the living room.

Dallas settled on the floor with the dump truck. Lesley curled up on the sofa beside West. He reached for her hand, linking their fingers.

"West, if I tell you something, will you promise not to get mad?" she asked in a soft undertone, which was unnecessary. The truck's sound effects were loud enough to muffle her words from Dallas.

"I hate it when women say that." He shook his head. "Okay, I promise."

"I am not at my best in unsettled conditions. I live by rules and a schedule, and when something happens to disrupt my life, I know I overreact. I won't ask again what your plans are."

West started to say something, but she held up her hand. "Let me finish. Please, I just want to ask you to let me know as soon as you've decided."

Again he opened his mouth, and again she held up her hand. This time she accompanied the gesture with a shake of her head. "Don't answer now. I don't want you to. Just think about it."

"Think about what?" asked Dallas, climbing onto the sofa, squirming until he had pushed them apart. "Now we can all hold hands," he said, fitting the action to the words.

West left a short time later. As he opened the back door to let himself out, he was startled to hear Eunice speak. "You're good with him."

He turned, his hand on the doorknob. She stood on the other side of the room. She was folding napkins and placing them in an open drawer. "What?"

"I said, you're good with Dallas." The older woman continued her rhythmic movements, not looking at him. "Patient, tolerant—things like that."

"Thank you, Eunice," he said. "Good night."

Lesley let herself into the silent house. She wondered idly where Dallas and Eunice were. She dropped her bag on the counter and headed for the refrigerator, which held a calendar and notepad. It was their message center.

Neither she nor Eunice ever left for more than a few minutes without writing a note to the other.

No note. Odd. But they'd be back soon. She glanced at her watch. One forty-five.

Two hours later, her hands were shaking so hard she had to punch buttons three times to get the correct number for the police.

The woman who answered was not cooperative at first, informing her that she had to wait twenty-four hours to report a missing person. But then Lesley told the woman that one of the persons was only three years old.

In ten minutes she was sitting on the sofa with a uniformed officer. He took descriptions, snapshots and notes.

Then he asked about the father of the child.

She was stunned that she hadn't thought of West. She tried to explain the situation to the poor man, who was more confused with each word she uttered.

"Let me get this straight," he said. "You adopted the child three years ago."

"Almost three and a half," she corrected.

"The father shows up a few weeks ago, claiming not to have known of the child's existence. You and he have—um—been seeing each other."

"Yes, we're trying to work this out so as to cause the least amount of damage to Dallas."

"You are sure that he wouldn't have taken the child?"

"Yes—no. I don't know. I don't think so. But where is the nanny, Eunice? We always leave notes or call each other if we aren't where we say we'll be. Always."

"Because of your television exposure? I suppose that would make you nervous of kidnapping threats."

"Partly. But our main reason is that we both love Dallas. Knowing that he is safe is vital to us. What if there has been an accident?"

His mention of a kidnapping threat had reminded her of the agency, but she wouldn't confuse him more by adding that to the mix right now.

"Why don't you see if you can get in touch with Mr. Chadwick?"

"Yes. I'll call him." She went to the telephone in the kitchen.

The officer followed. "Where is his office?"

She gave him directions as she punched in numbers. Her hand was shaking visibly. "The line is busy," she said helplessly to the man.

"Keep trying. I'm going over there. I'll check in with the precinct on my car radio." He scribbled a number and his name on a sheet of paper and gave it to her. "I have your number. If you have to get in touch with me, call the precinct. They'll patch you through."

West was beaming with the pride of fatherhood. He watched fondly as Dallas bounced on the sofa in the waiting room. Betsy was cooing, and even the staid Mrs. Riddock was watching fondly, too, like a grandparent.

The comparison reminded him: Mrs. Davis was there to sign her latest will. She knew his parents well. She was eager to talk about Dallas. "He's the spittin' image of you at that age, West," she had said.

He had to get her alone, to ask her to keep quiet for a while. "He can read," he stated in an attempt to divert the subject.

"Ah, c'mon, West. He can read at three?" asked Luke.

"Well, he read all the stop signs between here and the airport."

West had gotten an SOS from Eunice just before lunch. Her aunt in Virginia had suffered what the doctors believed to be a heart attack.

Eunice was listed as next of kin and she had to get on a plane as soon as possible. The woman had no one else. "The doctor assures me that it wasn't a severe attack, but at seventy-four any attack is severe," Eunice had said. "There's a plane leaving at one. I've tried and I can't get in touch with Lesley. I wondered if you would mind—"

"I'll be right there, Eunice. Don't worry about anything except your aunt. I can take care of Dallas until Lesley gets home. I'll also take you to the airport."

"There's no need. I'll phone for a cab."

"I insist. You pack and I'll pick you both up in say—" he glanced at his watch "—thirty minutes." He had a couple of calls to make.

"Thank you, West."

He was proud of himself when he remembered to borrow Luke's sedan. Maybe he was beginning to think like a father.

He was even more proud that the child had not shown the least apprehension when West had gone to the house to pick them up.

When Eunice got out of the car at the curbside check-in, however, West held his breath for fear Dallas would protest.

But he didn't. Instead he waved goodbye to Eunice from his car seat. Then he asked West what they were going to do.

"Do?" He hadn't thought about that. He could take Dallas home. Eunice had given him her key to Lesley's house. Or... "Would you like to see where I work? The office is on our way to your house." And he needed to rearrange some afternoon appointments.

"'Kay," Dallas agreed calmly. They talked for a few minutes, then Dallas fell asleep, just as he had done at the lake. He simply closed his eyes, and he was out. West smiled into the rearview mirror. Then he released a big breath of relief.

Because of the notice Dallas was receiving, the office visit had lasted longer than expected. "Come on, hot-shot. It's time to go home. I'm sure your mother is missing you."

"Bye, Dallas. Come back to see us, you hear?" Mrs. Riddock said. Her eyes were suspiciously bright. "He's a fine boy West," she added in an aside.

West could hardly believe the woman's tender reaction. He was one of the few who knew her to be kind, a side she rarely revealed during business hours. She could inhibit the most belligerent client with a look, but this child had her acting as if honey ran in her veins instead of the ice water everyone except West suspected.

Dallas simply grinned as though all the attention were his due. "I will. Bye, everybody."

West took the boy's hand and was about to leave, when a very young cop walked in. He looked at the man with the child.

"Are you West Chadwick?"

"Yes, I am. Can I help you?"

"I have to question you about a report of a possible kidnapping."

West felt the blood drain from his face. "Lesley?" he whispered.

The young officer nodded.

West felt his knees weaken. Automatically, he picked Dallas up in his arms and held him tightly. "Oh, my God," he breathed.

Luke, who had been about to show a client into his own office, excused himself and crossed the room quickly to stand beside West. "Officer, I'm Mr. Chadwick's partner. What's going on?"

His tension communicated itself to Dallas, who started to whimper, then to cry.

Mrs. Riddock stepped forward to take him from West. "Don't cry, precious. I'll let you play with my computer again."

The officer interceded, moving between West and the woman. "Ma'am? Is that Dallas MacDonald?"

"Yes. We'll sit right there at my desk while you explain."

"I'm not here to explain. I'm here to ask questions," said the officer. His eyes were hard.

"Well, we certainly won't run away, will we, precious?" she said tersely. She walked around the man as though he were a chair in her path and took the weeping child. As she crossed to her desk, she whispered to him and stroked his back consolingly.

Dallas stopped crying, but his whimpering breath came in hiccups. His eyes didn't leave West.

The officer took a notepad from a buttoned pocket in his tunic. "We had a call from a Lesley MacDonald, saying her nanny and baby were missing. Now, I presume that is the child. Where is—" he consulted his pad again "—Mrs. Eunice Delaney?"

The color returned to West's face in a surge of immense relief . . . an emotion that quickly changed to animosity. "You mean—are you saying that Lesley MacDonald is *not* the one who's missing?"

"No, sir, she's—"

"Right here," said an angry voice from the doorway. Lesley stomped across the room and plucked Dallas from the startled woman who held him.

"Mommy! You're here," Dallas said in delight. "I learned to work a 'puter. With a mouse. Not a mouse with a tail—"

Lesley placed her hand firmly on Dallas's back, effectively cutting him off. She whirled on West like a tiger protecting her cub. "What do you *mean* taking my child without my permission?" she snapped.

Mrs. Riddock and Luke, even the officer and everyone else in the office, stared at the suddenly frozen tableau.

"You didn't find my note," West said, finally breaking the silence. It was a statement, not a question.

"There *was* no note."

Luke, who could sense the beginnings of another scene, moved quickly, herding them all into his office. He shut the door. "Do you think we could straighten this out like mature adults?" he inquired, poker-faced. "Lesley, West got a call from Dallas's nanny, saying that her aunt in Virginia was ill."

West stepped forward. "Eunice's aunt had a heart attack. She couldn't get to you, so she called me. What was the poor woman to do?" He planted his fists on his hips. "This is the kind of thing that happens when a mother is hell-bent on a career. You can't take care of everything without someone suffering for it."

"I've done all right without your help so far."

Luke held up a hand. "West, why don't you let me finish the story?" He turned back to Lesley. "West took Eunice to the airport to catch the first plane out and brought Dallas back here. He was just leaving to go to your house, when this officer arrived."

Dallas put his hands on her cheeks and turned Lesley's face toward him. He looked worried. "Wes' wote a note and I hepped him."

Lesley sank into a chair, suddenly boneless. "I'll swear there wasn't a note, was there, Officer?"

The man shrugged. "I didn't see one."

"Well, I left one on the refrigerator. I wrote it while Eunice packed." West voiced each word, clearly and staccato. He ignored the dried tears on her face. "And neither Luke nor me appreciates you and this officer storming in here accusing me of kidnapping in front of our staff and clients. You could have called."

"The line was busy," she countered with a belligerent thrust of her chin.

"We have four rollover lines. If one is busy the next one rings. They are seldom all busy."

"Are you calling me a liar?" Again she turned to the policeman for backup. "Officer—"

"West thought it was you who'd been kidnapped, Lesley," put in Luke, earning himself a glare from his partner.

Lesley was suddenly still; her eyes flew to West's stony face. "You thought it was me?"

"Yeah," Luke continued. "Scared the tar out of him."

The officer spoke up. "You seem to have a misunderstanding here that can be resolved without me," he said.

No one answered him. "Ms. MacDonald?" he prompted.

West had thought it was she who was in danger? Lesley was speechless. She seemed to be submerged in a viscous liquid and everything she saw around her was blurred and distorted. West had been afraid on her behalf. He had cared. She wasn't able to think straight. "Oh, yes, Officer," she said faintly. "I—uh—"

The officer waited, but she didn't seem able to go on.

The explanation and West's accusation had brought back all her inner turmoil and self-doubts, her fears that she might shortchange Dallas. She had overreacted—*oh, boy,* had she overreacted. And worst of all, as she stood there with her son in her arms, she had suddenly discovered that she might be...she probably *was* falling in love with West Chadwick.

She was thankful when Luke took the young officer aside.

"I'm sure Ms. MacDonald apologizes for putting you in the middle of this mix-up. Do you—can you—what do you have to do with my help? Fill out a report?"

"I think I can manage to lose this one," said the officer in disgust. "My lieutenant would probably never believe me anyway."

West's anger was down to a dull simmer point as he followed Lesley home. Her stubbornness alone had caused the scene in the office. All she had to do was trust him.

But no, dammit. She was afraid to ask for help, afraid to need or depend on anyone. He knew her background accounted for part of her insecurity. But she was no longer a child, shuffled from place to place. She had a home and a son. She had a career. And she loved them all; they were of equal importance to her.

Too bad he couldn't equate that characteristic with his own mother.

He had a sudden thought. Unexpected and enlightening.

He parked behind her in the driveway and was out and around his car before she could get Dallas out of his seat. "I'll get him," he said. He unbuckled the car seat and picked up the child.

Lesley let him. She sighed; her shoulders slumped with weariness.

Dallas was beginning to fret. He wrapped his arm around West's neck and told him in a disdainful voice, "Forty pounds or four years old."

West drew back to look eye to eye with the child. "What?"

"That seat. I don't like it. Mommy's going to give it to the army."

"The army?" West was more confused.

Lesley explained in a tired voice. "He has to ride in the car seat until he weighs forty pounds or is four. Then we'll give it to the Salvation Army."

She'd forced herself to calm down over the course of the drive. Except for the sudden break in her adrenaline level, which left her fatigued, her emotions were on hold for the moment. She wasn't quite sure what she did feel for West, but whatever it was had been powerfully overwhelming for a few minutes there in his office. She believed she could face him with equanimity.

When she reached in her purse for her house keys, however, her hands trembled slightly. She realized that beneath the surface her feelings were still intense. The best thing to do now was to see if he really did leave a note and get rid of him.

She unlocked the door and let West and Dallas precede her into the back hallway.

"I'll show you the note, Mommy." Dallas squirmed to get down and West set him on his feet. He ran to the kitchen and toward the refrigerator.

West followed, looking puzzled. The spot where he'd left the note was empty.

Dallas sat on his heels in front of the appliance and tilted his head. "Here it is," he cried. He reached into the slim gap between the refrigerator and the counter and brought out a piece of paper. "My ball got stuck back there once," he said with a triumphant grin.

All the stuffing went out of Lesley. West hadn't lied. She turned to him, her lips parted, but she had no idea what to say.

Before she could speak he reached out a hand and cupped her face. His fingers were warm. He smiled sadly.

"Don't say anything. Your first concern was for your child. I blew up at the office. But I'm very glad to know you think of him first, and to hell with causing a scene. Cause a hundred scenes. If I could have chosen a mother for my child, that would have been the first criterion."

She shook her head. His anger had completely disappeared. There was something else in his expression— a look of melancholy or wistfulness that touched her deep inside, where her newly discovered feelings lay. "I'm not sure I understand," she said softly.

"My mother would never have made a scene," he elaborated, his voice toneless.

"Your mother?" She remembered from unexplained comments that there was something askew about his relationship with his parents. But she wasn't aware of details.

"Why don't you make a pot of coffee and we'll talk about it?"

Dallas, still holding the paper, watched the two adults with interest, but at West's suggestion he frowned. "I'm hungry," he declared, dropping the note on the floor. "I don't want coffee."

Both Lesley and West laughed. If the laughter held a note of desperation, neither of them said anything.

"Okay, sweetheart, I'll feed you first."

West retrieved the note and laid it on the table.

"I want a 'loney sandwich and chips. And—"

"And milk," she finished for him.

"Chocolate milk," he demanded, but his eyes were wide and innocent, as though he were wondering if he could get away with it.

"Chocolate milk," she conceded.

A few minutes later he was seated at the table, eating his sandwich. Lesley had put on the coffee, and as they waited for it to drip through, she remembered that she had to call Blanche immediately.

"Abe can handle the morning program alone. With any luck the nanny service will have a substitute available," she told him as she punched in the numbers. "If so, I can get to the studio before lunch."

West watched, but he tuned out her conversation. The late-afternoon sun streamed through the windows and painted her shining auburn hair with streaks of amber. Her tailored sea-green dress was a mass of wrinkles. She had eaten off all her lipstick. But the lines of concern and fear around her eyes and mouth had smoothed. She was in the kitchen of her own home. Her child was safe. She appeared to have gotten a second wind.

He thought she had never looked more beautiful. He wasn't sure why she seemed always to have this effect on him when they were in her kitchen. Once again, he felt himself becoming aroused. And there sat Dallas.

So he joined the child at the table.

When the coffee was ready, Lesley poured West and her a cup and sat down, too. "Tell me," she said.

He hesitated, as though choosing his words carefully. "Long before I was his age, I began to call the cook 'Mama.' I must have sensed that the poor woman was embarrassed to tears, so I stopped." His smile twisted slightly. "I tried out the name on the maid, the butler, the gardener, everyone. None of them seemed to like it.

"Finally, when I was old enough to understand, my parents straightened me out. However, they preferred that I not call anyone 'Mama.' They wanted to be known as 'Mother' and 'Father.'"

Lesley had felt a lump grow thick in her throat as he spoke. His voice was low and emotionless, indicating just how affected he was. "Oh, West," she said.

"Don't feel sorry for me." His voice was a growl, drawing Dallas's gaze.

He smiled gently at the child and lightened his pitch deliberately. "What was it you said? They paid all my bills. Besides, all that was many years ago. We get along now, as long as we don't see too much of one another."

But at what cost? thought Lesley. "We get along" was a far cry from "I love them."

"Do they know about Dallas?" She had wanted to ask the question several times but had postponed it for one reason or another. She wasn't sure why now had seemed an appropriate time.

"No, but I have no doubt they'll find out. When they do, you'll be inundated. They'll preempt your life if you let them."

"Don't worry about me. I can take care of myself."

His low chuckle held no humor. "You'd be a babe in the woods to them. You wouldn't even know what was happening. They are a charming couple. You know that—you've met them. And, honey, they are accustomed to getting their way—charmingly, of course."

He'd called her "honey." Her heart gave a jump at the endearment. She kept her voice even. "You don't know me very well if you think I'd let them."

All at once she had his full attention. "But I'm beginning to," he assured her.

His voice dropped to its lowest pitch, the one that sent shivers down her spine.

"Know you."

"Does this mean we're 'an item'?" asked Dallas, interceding for his own share of attention.

"A what?" exclaimed his mother.

"An item," he repeated. "Like a sat-a-light report from L.A. When people sit together to eat."

"The Hollywood segment," Lesley said, rolling her eyes.

West fought off a laugh. "I guess we are an item."

"You an' me an' Mommy." Dallas pushed his plate back, empty of chips and half his sandwich. He drained the glass of chocolate milk, dribbling a bit. "I'm ready to go to sleep."

"You have to have a bath first." She wiped Dallas's mouth with his napkin and turned to West. "Do you want to wait while I—"

He had already begun to shake his head. "I have to go," he said almost sharply. "I'll check in with you tomorrow. Call if you need me. Good night. 'Night, Dallas."

"'Night, Wes'."

She and Dallas watched him flee to the hallway. He didn't really run, but that was the impression he left with her.

"Is Wes' in a hurry?" Dallas asked.

The back door closed firmly. "Yes, he must be," answered his mother, reflecting on the hasty departure.

West breathed in the fresh air. An idea had followed their conversation and had sent him bolting from the scene.

They were an item, and as soon as his parents found out about Dallas, they would have one goal and one goal only.

Marriage. For West and Lesley.

They weren't in love—though there was a vibrant sensual awareness between them that could probably serve as a substitute. She felt it, too. It was amusing to observe her lose her cool. She had two signs that he could read clearly: she changed the subject abruptly and she started talking a mile a minute.

Not to mention the way her lips softened against his, the way she melted in his arms.

He was surprised that the idea of marriage didn't scare the hell out of him, though he wasn't enamored of the notion. He had a long list of reasons to avoid wedding vows, a list that had evolved through the years into a chiseled stone tablet.

What did scare him was the thought that she would marry him for Dallas's sake—only.

Eunice called a short time after Lesley finished putting Dallas to bed. Her aunt was going to need her for a week or so.

"It wasn't a heart attack, thank goodness. They're letting her go home tomorrow. She wants me to hire someone for her, but she's not a wealthy woman, Lesley."

Lesley felt her stomach drop, but she kept her voice light. "Of course you must stay with her, Eunice. Please don't worry about us. I'm taking the morning off to call the service and see about a substitute."

"Just make sure they know it's a temporary job," Eunice said adamantly. She gave Lesley the numbers of the hospital and her aunt's home. Then she asked, "May I speak to Dallas? I don't want him to think I've abandoned him."

"Would you believe, he's already in bed? He missed his nap. I'll have him call you tomorrow."

"Was everything all right today? You found West's note?"

"Yes, I found it." When she thought back over the day, she almost laughed. But she knew Eunice would hear and immediately identify the hysteria in her laugh.

"Don't worry. You take care of your aunt and yourself."

Lesley hung up the telephone. Drat! No one was to blame for this dilemma, but a dilemma it was. Dallas was so attached to his Newness he wasn't going to like this at all.

She had her hand on the light switch, when the telephone rang again. "Hello," she said.

"Ms. MacDonald, this is your adopted son's father," said the voice. But the voice did not belong to West.

At nine the next morning, Lesley walked into Blanche's office at the studio, holding Dallas's hand and carrying a net bag full of toys.

"You couldn't find a nanny," Blanche said.

"I haven't tried yet. If we can get one of the assistants to watch him in my office just while we're on the air—" She broke off.

Blanche took a long look at her friend. "Sit," she ordered. She took Dallas, settled him on the floor with his big, fancy truck and then turned back to Lesley. "What's happened?" she asked.

Lesley had explained about Eunice when she called yesterday, so Blanche knew her baby-sitting problem. "What else?"

This morning she knew there was no way to account for her look of nervous exhaustion. "I didn't sleep well," she said.

"You look like you didn't sleep at all."

"Not much." She hugged her body. "Oh, Blanche, I had a call from a man who said that he was Dallas's father, but it wasn't West. I haven't told you about the adoption agency and West's private detective." She straightened, knowing her explanation was garbled, to say the least. "West said there is something odd going on with that agency. My suspicions are aroused now—the caller suggested he might settle for money—and I want to reopen my investigation."

"We'll discuss it. But not right now."

"The man also didn't seem to know that Valerie had died. Oh, Blanche, that terrified me. He's a fraud. How do I know what else he might be?"

Abe came in while she was trying to sort her tumultuous thoughts and bring them into rational order. So she had to begin again.

"Why didn't you tell us all this was going on?"

"Kidnapping?"

"You've been trying to manage all this by yourself?"

"The police? Why didn't you call me?"

The complete story took almost a half hour.

At the end of that time, her friends were staring at her. She soothed their hurt feelings.

At last Blanche checked her watch. "I'll find someone to take care of Dallas. Abe can fill you in on the schedule for the lunch show. We'll conclude this later. And in the meantime, sweetie, you know that the studio is no place for a child," she added gently. She put her hands on her hips. "But you're not going back to that house alone tonight. Do you hear me?" she finished determinedly.

"Going home isn't the problem. I can screen calls through the answering machine."

"And stay up all night watching the doors and windows."

"I didn't say I had done that," Lesley protested.

"You didn't have to. Just look in a mirror."

Once Lesley and Abe had left her office, Blanche thought for a very brief minute. She picked up the telephone. "Get me West Chadwick," she said to her secretary. "He's a lawyer here in town. I need to speak to him as soon as possible."

Chapter 9

"That's a wrap," said Blanche from the control booth. "Good show," she added, which was as close as she ever got to effusive praise.

The program had gone very smoothly; Lesley and Abe grinned at each other and she blew out a breath of enormous relief.

"You were as good as you've ever been," Abe complimented. "Maybe you'd better start going on more often without rehearsal."

"Not a chance. I'm a nervous wreck. Besides, you carried the show."

They unclipped the microphones and stood.

Lesley froze at the first glimpse of West. He was standing behind the glass in the production booth, holding Dallas. Blanche must have called him. Drat!

"Is that Blanche's new boyfriend?" asked Abe. "He doesn't look too happy."

She lifted a hand and Dallas waved enthusiastically. West watched her steadily, but he didn't smile. "No, he doesn't, does he? That's West Chadwick."

"The one . . . ?"

"Yes." Drat, she'd made West mad again. She'd thought about phoning him herself last night; she really had. She probably should have, since the stranger claimed to be Dallas's father. But the call had come very late.

Would he accept that as an excuse?

Of course not. Neither would she, had their places been reversed. And wasn't that the standard he seemed to have set for her? At least she was learning that his temper never lasted very long.

She sighed and headed for the booth, muttering about friends who thought they knew what was best for you.

Abe followed. "I'm here if you need me," he reassured her.

"I'll be fine."

"I don't know. That's one big dude." Abe, who himself was a substantial six foot plus, gave a mock shudder of fear.

She laughed and placed her hand on his arm. "Thanks," she said, meaning it. "Come on, I'll introduce you to Dallas's father."

West met them in the hall. He looked at her hand still resting on Abe's arm. His eyes took on a chilling glitter. "Blanche explained everything. Why didn't you call me?" he demanded.

"Mommy, Wes' came to play with me." He held out his arms to her.

She took her son and sat him on her hip, but spoke to West. "I thought about it, but it was very late. And I didn't want you to feel that you had to be responsible for us." She introduced Abe, and the men shook hands almost as an afterthought.

"I want down," Dallas proclaimed.

"No, you can't run around in the studio." Lesley's answer was a reflex. Her gaze remained on West.

"Will you excuse us?" West said after a moment, turning Lesley aside with a hand on her shoulder.

She started to protest his high-handedness, but Abe waved them off. "Sure. I know you have a lot to talk about."

Blanche joined Abe. She was silent as Lesley looked back at her, but her eyes spoke volumes, the theme of which was *I'm sorry, I know you hate to lean on anyone. But I had to do this.*

Lesley stopped where she was. "Blanche, thank you for. calling West to help me." Her gaze moved from Blanche to Abe. "We'll be all right now."

She smiled, her composure intact. Blanche and Abe were the only ones who realized what a big step it was for her to admit she needed help.

"You've got it," said West.

Well, maybe her friends were not the only ones.

"We need to get clothes and a few things from the house," Lesley said as they left the station.

It appeared that Blanche and West had worked out a schedule without her. She was going to spend a few days with him. At least until she could find a nanny.

She stopped suddenly, and West, who had taken Dallas, almost knocked her down.

Keeping a firm hold on the child, he steadied her, too.

"West, are you sure you have room for us in your condo?" she asked.

West found himself pacified, even gratified, by Lesley's admission that it was difficult for a mother to do everything alone. Suddenly he knew—but maybe most important he understood—how much of an effort it took for her to say the words to her friends.

She wasn't at all like his mother. But she should have called him.

"I'm sure. I have two bedrooms. You don't mind sharing a room with Dallas, do you?"

He was eager to have them at his place. He wasn't sure why—other than the obvious: they would be alone much of the time. Maybe they could accomplish the bonding she talked about so much. He wasn't inclined to analyze his feelings beyond that juncture.

I'd rather share with you, Lesley thought. Then she chastized herself. It would be hard enough to hide her deepest feelings for him without adding intimacy to the mix. Especially the thunder and lightning that passed for intimacy between them.

She could not forget the hunger of his lips, the strength of his hard body, the feel of his smooth skin, even across the gap of ongoing disagreements that had opened once again. "No, of course not," she said.

But it wasn't going to be easy being around him in a personal setting.

"I'm hungry," Dallas said.

West smiled at Lesley, then down at the child, who walked between them, holding both their hands. "He began regular announcements that he was ready to eat an hour ago," West told her. "Blanche scrounged up a stale peanut-butter cracker. But it didn't satisfy him for very long. Why don't we go out for lunch?"

"Yea-a," Dallas said.

"After we eat we can swing by your place." *And by then I hope Alex will have worked her magic.*

He had made a few calls from his office as soon as Blanche informed him of the situation at the station. One had been to Will; he'd gotten the detective's answering machine.

Another of them had been to Alex. He asked her for information about buying a couple of beds for his second bedroom. She had to know why, of course.

"West, are you talking about the room that's full of exercise equipment?" she'd asked, when he told her that he needed them in a hurry.

Lord, he'd been picturing it as a bedroom; he'd forgotten that the room held two weight machines, a rowing machine and a stationary bicycle. "Yeah," he said. "I need someone to move stuff out, too."

"All right."

He could almost hear her mind turning over.

"David can take care of that." She volunteered her son without a thought.

"You'd better ask him first."

"He'll do it."

He was grateful and told her so. "It's convenient to have someone in the family with a new pickup."

Family—it was just an expression, wasn't it?

David, Alexandra's son, Luke's stepson, had turned sixteen this year. A pickup truck was the vehicle of choice among his peers.

"You know, you could rent the beds, West. In fact, you can rent a whole room of furniture and the company will deliver."

"No," he said without hesitation. "Spend whatever you have to." For the first time in his life, he had displayed the same arrogance his parents would have shown had someone suggested such a thing. "I mean what's necessary."

"I know what you mean, West," Alex said fondly.

Lesley and Dallas had to have new beds to sleep on. "I guess I do need more furniture to turn it into a guest room. A couple of chests with drawers and a table or two. Nice ones."

Alex had thought for a minute. "Would you trust me to take care of this for you?"

"Of course," he'd answered, amazed that she had to ask. "Luke has a key." At one time they had all lived in the same building, and she knew her way around. "I hate to ask this of you, Alex, but I don't know where else to turn. Are you sure it won't be too much trouble?"

"Trouble? To spend someone else's money? It'll be fun," she said, chuckling. "I have a friend in the decorating business I can call. How long do I have?"

He glanced at his watch. "It's ten now. I'm heading to the station to take care of Dallas for a while. Lesley goes on the air at twelve. She usually gets through at one."

"Has she packed?"

"I don't think so."

"Take them to lunch first. Then she'll need to pick up their clothes. I think I can have things fairly straight by three or three-thirty."

He'd grinned. "Alex, you are wonderful. Roses won't be a sufficient thank-you present this time. What do you want?"

"Are you kidding?" Her laugh was elated. "I want to meet these two."

"Luke's been talking."

"Of course. He tells me everything—well, almost. I can't wait to see them. Even David is curious."

So that was why she was so certain when she'd volunteered her son.

She went on, humor in her voice. "I understand Ms. MacDonald can make you lose your cool."

"Well—we've had some misunderstandings."

"From what I hear, that's the understatement of the year," she put in dryly. "But I don't mean to make light of it, West. I know the situation is serious."

"Yes, it is. I hope we can get through it without a major battle." He paused, deliberately easing into a teasing tone. "You've seen her on TV?"

"Naturally."

"Then you know she has red hair."

He smiled to himself. "Red" didn't describe it; it was the color of the setting sun over water when clouds hung low, the dark-red color that resembled a fine claret. And the way the sun shone upon it was dazzling. He shook himself out of his musings. "You know what they say about redheads?" he finished offhandedly.

"I presume you mean the temper thing? I know blondes are supposedly bimbos, too, but I've found it doesn't always hold true, haven't you?" Alex answered sweetly. Too sweetly.

"Of course, Alex. Sorry," West apologized, decently chastized. Alex was a blonde.

When they arrived at the condo, Alex, David and Luke were waiting.

Dallas, who was happily holding West's hand, pulled away. He wrapped his arms around Lesley's legs. "Take me," he said when he saw the strangers. She hoisted him up and he buried his face in her neck.

Introductions were made. Then West turned to his partner and friend. "Did you close down the office?"

"Yeah," Luke answered. "I gave everyone the afternoon off."

"And you'll cover for me a while longer?"

Luke clapped his friend's shoulder with a sound slap. "Sure. As Alex reminded me, I owe you big time."

West had taken on Luke's work as well as his own in the downtown law firm where they used to work a few years ago when Alex and her son had been in danger and Luke wouldn't leave them alone.

"You don't owe me a thing," he said gruffly.

Lesley was amazed by the affection West showed to these three people. She'd never seen him so unconstrained. This was the kind of family he'd needed, and obviously had found in the Quinlans. He might not recognize the relationship, but he had bonded with them.

Alex was a beautiful blonde, and her son, David, seemed to be beyond that awkward-teen stage. He was a nice-looking young man.

She herself felt suddenly shy, a rare condition for her. She smiled a lot and rubbed Dallas's back reassuringly as they reached the first-name stage.

Alex separated herself from the men and nudged her to the side. "I'm really very happy to meet you, Lesley. I enjoy the shows you do with Abe Mandina." There was no doubting her sincerity.

"Thank you. I'll tell him you said so." She didn't know what else to say. She had not been at such a loss for many, many years. "How old is David?"

To be truthful, she was jealous of West's obvious kinship to them, his easy attachment. Although she was on the receiving end of his sensual interest, he wasn't as easy with her as he was with this family.

"Sixteen," Alex answered.

Lesley had almost forgotten she'd asked the question. "He's quite handsome." Lord, how trite she sounded.

Alex grinned. "So is yours, I think," she said. Her voice was low and pleasant. She tickled Dallas's waist. "If he would look at me I could tell for sure."

Dallas turned to peer out at her with one eye.

"Dallas must like to play peekaboo," Alex teased, smiling.

Dallas inserted two fingers into his mouth, but he returned her smile and raised his head.

"Oh, my," breathed Alex. "He *is*—handsome."

"Like his father," Lesley finished for her.

If Alex was surprised, she didn't let it show. Instead she touched Dallas's shining blond hair. "See David over there? He's my little boy, like you're your mommy's."

Dallas eyed David. "He's not very little."

"Not now, but he was when he was your age."

Dallas straightened, watching David as he carried in the last load from Lesley's car into the condo. He then returned to the porch to say something to West before coming toward them.

"Will I ever be as big as you?" Dallas blurted, his blue eyes rounded.

"Sure you will," David answered easily, shoving his hands into the pockets of his jeans. "I hear you like trucks. Would you like to see mine?"

"Oh, *yes*," Dallas declared, as though his greatest wish had been granted. He squirmed to get down.

David looked to Lesley for her permission. She thanked him and set the child on his feet. "Hold David's hand in the parking lot," she warned.

Alex smiled fondly at her son, then at Lesley. "He'll grow up overnight," she said, ruefully, almost sadly. Then she changed the subject. "Let me tell you about the things I found in West's refrigerator."

Lesley listened, her eyes glistening with amusement, as Alex listed the foods a gourmet might consider necessities. "He does have a nice-looking ham and a loaf of bread," Alex finished. "But that's about it."

"I doubt that Dallas will eat pâte de fois gras. He will eat cheese, but I've never tried Brie on him."

"If there's anything he particularly likes, I can go to the store for you. Or David can."

At the sound of an exuberant squeal, they turned. "Look, Mom. Look at me!" Dallas jumped up and down in the bed of the pickup truck. David was close, on guard.

Lesley waved and turned back to Alex. "Thanks, Alex." Her shyness had been swiftly overcome by Alex's warmth and kindness. "You've all been so nice. But as far as groceries, the market is Dallas's favorite place. I wouldn't dare shop without him."

"Well, I guess I'll get my men out of here so you can settle in. Please call if you need me. Our home number is scribbled on the front of the phone book."

"I will. Thanks again."

Luke approached at that moment. "Ready?" he asked his wife. Then he repeated her thoughts. "We'd better let these two get settled in."

Alex grinned at Lesley. "We're on the same wavelength. Isn't that great?"

Indeed it was great. She wondered if she would ever have a relationship like theirs.

Lesley watched as they drove away. A few minutes later David returned a deliriously happy Dallas to her and also left.

"Do you think he would like kiwi? Or what about avocados?" asked West as they made their way through the produce department.

"Bananas and carrots—these little tiny ones," answered Lesley, dropping the items in the grocery cart.

West pushed, with Dallas buckled into the seat. "He has to eat something green, doesn't he?"

"A little taste of lettuce in a salad when I demand it. And he likes canned green beans. Believe me, that's it."

"Okay. Does he like cereal? Pasta?"

He looked relieved when she nodded, but then she added, "Macaroni and cheese is one of his favorites."

"Good God," he muttered.

Lesley laughed. "And don't forget peanut butter and jelly."

He grinned. "I have those—they're staples."

By the time they reached the checkout counter, Dallas had pointed out a few other things that he considered staples: chocolate syrup for his milk, barbecue-flavored potato chips, and cookies. "Any kind," he told West amiably.

"Graham crackers or vanilla wafers," said his mother.

The guest room was comfortable, if a bit strange. Hunter-green comforters covered the twin beds, one of which had been pushed into the corner for Dallas. A varnished wicker trunk with brass fittings and a lovely lamp sat between the beds. Two matching chests of drawers were on the opposite wall—antiques, if Lesley wasn't mistaken. A dark bentwood rocker, also antique, was angled in a corner and a crooknecked floor lamp sat next to the chair.

The odd thing about the room was that there were no finishing touches. No curtains or drapes, no pictures on the walls, no knickknacks at all.

And all the other rooms in the condo were decorated with contemporary furnishings. This was definitely traditional.

It was as though everything in this room had been moved in today.

She suspected that it had. And she suspected that Alex was responsible. As she put Dallas to bed that night, she wondered what the room had been used for before.

When she joined West in the living room, she asked. She was surprised when he admitted that his exercise equipment was now residing in the Quinlans' garage.

"My exercise schedule is erratic, to say the least, so I used that room when I couldn't get out to run or play golf or tennis."

She moved to the floor-length window that overlooked the common area of the complex. A fenced pool was dark now; beyond that were lighted tennis courts. Lovely plantings, benches, too, filled a central space. The condos, and thus the road, formed a large, enclosing oval of several acres. "Well, maybe we won't be here too long. You can have your room back."

"Don't say that, Lesley," West commented. He came from behind and wrapped his arms around her. "I want you to feel comfortable here for as long as you'll stay." He paused. "You've had a difficult few days."

She heard the apology in his voice as she let herself lean against him. The terrifying phone call, the sleepless night, the harrowing day were catching up with her. It felt good to be held against his strong, stable frame. "I'm exhausted," she admitted.

"I told you I want you to be comfortable here. A good night's sleep is what you need." He tried to sound upbeat. "We can talk tomorrow."

"We need to talk tonight. How are we going to work out our schedule? And did you tell your detective about the phone call I got?"

"Will was out, but don't worry about the schedule. Luke and I have discussed it. I'll be here in the mornings until you get home."

With his promise, West felt her relax fully. He wasn't certain why he felt so at ease with them here. He was accustomed to living alone and valued his privacy. He'd known women, had some serious thoughts about one or two of them, but he'd never been serious enough to have a woman move in with him.

This was different.

She was warm; her warmth seeped into his own body. He hadn't been aware that he was cold. He closed his eyes, put his chin atop her head and inhaled deeply. "You always smell so good," he murmured.

She raised her hands to his arms, her fingers stroking lightly against the hair on his forearms. Her touch was gentle, but provocative to his susceptible libido. He felt himself stir. He dipped his head, kissed the side of her neck.

"Where's my Hop?" Dallas asked from the door to the living room.

Lesley could have cried.

Or cursed.

She did neither.

She sighed. It was her own fault that Hop had been forgotten. Her thoughts had been on the telephone call, Eunice and West. Mostly West.

Though the old stuffed rabbit wasn't a regular requirement at home anymore, she knew without a doubt that Dallas wouldn't go to sleep in a strange bed without Hop. "I put it on the kitchen counter by the door so I wouldn't forget it. I'll have to—"

"No, you will not," West interrupted. He turned her and put his hands firmly on her upper arms. She lifted her palm to his chest. He went on, though the imprint of her fingers felt like a red-hot cattle brand. "You will unwind, run yourself a tub, get ready for bed, and I'll go. Where are you keys?"

"I hate to ask it of you," Lesley protested.

"You aren't asking. I'm offering."

She smiled her relief and rested her forehead on his broad chest for a brief moment.

"Is my mom sick?"

When Dallas pulled on his trousers leg, he had to release her.

Lesley summoned a smile for her son. "No, sweetheart, I'm fine, just tired." She turned back to West. "Thank you. The keys are in my purse. I'll get them."

West sat in a chair and held out a hand to Dallas. "I'll be back in a few minutes with your Hop. But you'll be a good boy while I'm gone, won't you? Your mommy has had a long day."

Dallas nodded. "Okay. Can I watch TV till you get back?"

West lifted his shoulders in a shrug and concealed a smile as Lesley reentered the room. "You'll have to ask her."

"Forget it," Dallas muttered disgustedly.

"Good idea," Lesley said, raising a brow to her son. She handed West her key ring. "This is the key to the back hall. Hop is on the kitchen counter."

He took the key from her and dropped a kiss on her forehead. "I'll be back in a few minutes. The answering machine's on, so if you're in the tub..." Without warning an image of her naked in his bathtub appeared on the surface of his mind.

"I won't answer." Lesley wondered if he had a lot of women who called him. Probably so. Leggy blondes, petite brunettes. She could just picture them. He wouldn't *want* her to answer the phone.

West was afraid to speak for fear she would hear the arousal in his voice, so he nodded, pocketed her keys and hurried out the door.

She herded Dallas toward the bedroom. "Okay, big boy, back to bed," she said cheerfully, in an attempt to put all those other women out of her mind.

The door reopened.

"Hey—" West stuck his head in. He looked bemused as he asked, "What *is* a Hop?"

Blanche had insisted that Lesley skip the early-morning news again Wednesday. But she did want her back for the lunch show.

She was dressed for the show but had on no makeup when she pulled her car out of the parking lot. West, holding Dallas by the hand, waved from the porch. She waved back.

Dallas was quiet and looked doubtful, but he didn't cry, as Lesley had feared.

"So, here we are," said West, hunkering down next to the child.

Dallas stuck two fingers in his mouth and pulled his lower teeth down. His eyes were fixed warily on West. It was the same maneuver he'd used the first time West met him. West was learning that it meant "I'm making up my mind whether I like this arrangement or not."

"Me, too," West said, not realizing he'd spoken aloud until Dallas's eyes widened even more. He searched his mind for something to entertain the child. "Would you like to go for a walk?"

Dallas nodded. "I guess so."

"Okay. But I'm expecting a call. Let me get my phone and we'll walk." They headed for the center of the condo complex, which was deserted at this time of day.

Dallas was fascinated by everything. He thought it was one big playground, just for him. "But where are the swings?" he asked.

"They're in the park. This is another kind of playground. Mostly for grown-ups."

"Aren't there any children here?"

"Not many," West acknowledged. He was silent, but his thoughts continued. The few children who did live in the complex were in day care at this hour. The people he knew here usually began looking for a house as soon as they started a family. This wasn't a place to raise children.

"It's a nice place to run," observed Dallas hopefully.

West got the message, and the morning sun had dried the dew. He let go of the child's hand so he could sprint across the grass.

First Dallas was a plane, with all the appropriate sound effects. He ran, arms extended, as he made a large circle and came back to West.

West grinned. Then he himself was a horse, slapping his thigh while he yelled, "Giddyup." Dallas copied every move. They threw an imaginary football back and forth. They played for over an hour before West called time-out. Where in the world did the child get his energy? he wondered, not for the first time.

He was sitting on the grassy verge around the tennis courts, one forearm propped loosely over his flexed knee. Dallas was busy looking for bugs.

The phone in the back pocket of his jeans rang. It was Will. "Sorry I was out of town yesterday."

"That's okay." He filled the detective in on the telephone call Lesley had gotten. "The fellow made a stupid mistake this time when he said he was Dallas's father. I think he's screwed up."

"You think right. And this may give me some leverage to get the other parents to talk. I'll get back to you as soon as I can."

"Fine. Call or drop by. I'll be at home today."

"At home?"

"It's a long story."

"Mom! Here comes Mom!" Dallas squealed. "That's her car!"

Dallas had been watching and waiting beside the window. He'd insisted West move the table and serve his lunch there so he could see the parking lot. He sat on West's unabridged dictionary and a pillow. They had forgotten his booster seat. He was eating a hot dog, macaroni and cheese, and carrots.

West was sprawled in an easy chair, his long legs stretched bonelessly in front of him, his arms dangling over the padded arms of the chair.

Dallas dropped the hot dog, which rolled off the table. He scooted to the floor, his bottom dragging the pillow and the book with him. He ended up in a tangle, but he was apparently adept at freeing himself from tangles. He was up in an instant and out of the room. "Open up, Wes'," he demanded.

"Coming." West got slowly to his feet and followed him to the front door.

Lesley absorbed the blow of her child against her legs with the ease of long practice. "Hi, sweetheart." West looked like the very devil. "Have you been a good boy?" she asked, all the while keeping her gaze on West. His hair was tousled, his shirttail hanging loose, and he was barefoot.

"Yes, ma'am," Dallas answered politely.

She looked inquiringly at West.

"I'm so *very* glad to see you," he said. Without another word, he stepped forward and drew her into his arms.

Dallas was squirming between their legs, but Lesley surrendered to his hard hug with a delicious feeling of homecoming. "Did he give you any trouble?" she murmured against his shirt.

"No trouble. A few minor heart attacks, but other than that, he's been fine."

"I have to finish eating," said Dallas.

"Okay," she answered. But she tilted her head back to look up at West.

West tried to shrug. He didn't quite pull it off. "He really has been good. It's me. I didn't realize I was so out of shape."

Her smile was wide; the dimple showed up. "You haven't seen the television special about the professional football player who tried to follow a toddler around for one whole day, copying all the physical moves of the child? The football player gave out about ten-thirty in the morning."

That drew a smile from West. He turned her toward the living room. "If you're trying to make me feel better, you've got a long way to go. I feel like I'm a hundred years old." He hesitated. "But you know," he added thoughtfully, "I enjoyed it. He's quite a kid. And he certainly has some unique ideas. He saved a few of the more interesting bugs to show you."

"How thrilling," Lesley said dryly.

"Yeah. I talked him out of eating them all."

She laughed on cue. As they entered the living room, he kept his arm across her shoulder. She wasn't sure that he wasn't using her as a crutch, but that was fine with her. She loved the feeling of his lean, strong body close to hers.

"Want a hot dog, Mom?" Dallas asked.

"When did you decide to call me 'Mom'?" she asked curiously.

Dallas looked at her with a surprisingly mature expression. "David calls his mother 'Mom.'"

"I see."

"He says that's what big boys do," Dallas explained as he picked the hot dog off the floor and brought it toward his mouth.

"Throw that away," said West firmly. "Big boys don't eat things off the floor."

West held his breath. He had spoken without thinking and it was the first direct order he had ever given the child.

Dallas looked from West's face to his mother's, then at the half-eaten hot dog. The tension in the room was palpable.

No one spoke. West waited for Lesley to tell him to back off. But she didn't.

Dallas seemed to be thinking. "Okay," he said finally. He trotted into the kitchen, opened the door of the undersink cabinet and dropped the food in the garbage can.

West breathed again.

As did Lesley. "That was quick thinking," she said with admiration in her smile. "Big boys, huh?"

"Should be good for a few more incidents," West said at last, winking at her. "So, want some macaroni and cheese?"

Dallas was taking a nap. The condo was quiet. West had disappeared into his room, saying he had a couple of things to handle, via fax and modem, for the office. "Mrs. Riddock is fully capable of fending off impatient clients, but I don't want to lose them because they think I'd neglect their business."

Lesley was more impressed when he went on to explain his and Luke's purpose for leaving the big downtown firm. The partnership would assist the underdog, take on small cases, serve budding entrepreneurs. That had been their driving force from day one.

She was in the living room going over her notes for tomorrow's show, when the telephone on the table beside her began to ring. And ring and ring.

Where was West? He must have disconnected the answering machine. At last she picked it up. "Hello?"

"This is Will McCarty. May I speak to West Chadwick?"

"Just a minute, please," she said, wondering why West hadn't answered himself. He had an extension in his bedroom.

"West? Telephone," she called out as she walked down the hall toward his open bedroom door.

The large room, like the rest of the condo, was starkly contemporary. Here he had his desk and bookcases, a dresser, all in polished ebony or teakwood. The luxurious carpet was a smoky gray and felt plush beneath her bare toes.

She smiled at the sight before her.

West lay sprawled across a huge king-size bed, on his back, sound asleep. Clearly Dallas had worn him out. He had probably felt obliged to entertain the child every second.

Earlier he had held his breath, wondering if she would interfere when he told Dallas to do something. Not a chance. She'd liked his firm manner.

Before tomorrow she could clarify those parenting concepts for him. Adults had to band together if they wanted to maintain any kind of control. She chuckled as she moved forward.

In repose, his features were even more like Dallas's. His lashes, though darker, were as thick, his jaw as stubborn, his mouth...no, his mouth was that of a man, a very masculine man. A ribbon of warmth traveled up her spine.

She touched his shoulder, her fingers lingering there. "Telephone, West."

He opened his eyes and blinked up at her. That mouth curved into a sensual smile that turned her insides to hot jelly.

"Hi," he said huskily. He reached for her hand; his was warm and strong.

Lesley was tempted to let the man hang on the phone until he got tired of waiting. Instead she tugged at West's hand. "You didn't hear the phone ring. It's for you, a Will McCarty."

He looked confused for a moment, then he sat up, reaching for the extension on his bedside table. But he didn't let go of her hand. "Stay with me," he said, threading his fingers through hers, resting both their forearms on his hard thigh.

"Hello, Will." He talked for a few minutes, but she had no idea what was said. All she could think of was the softy, husky voice, the warmth that radiated from him, the compact feel of his thigh.

When he hung up he looked at her with breath-stealing tenderness. He tracked each of her fingers with the tips of his. Then he raised them to his lips. "That was the investigator I told you about. He wants to talk to you about the agency."

"All right," she whispered unsteadily. His nibbling kisses made her fingers tingle, her heart pound. She wondered what they would do to the rest of her.

His gaze fell to her mouth and she had to consciously stop herself from licking her lips.

He muttered a curse, but delivered a hard, fast kiss. It was all he would allow himself. "He'll be here in an hour to question you."

That isn't long enough. And Dallas will wake up soon. He appeared as frustrated as she felt.

Chapter 10

Will made Lesley go over *exactly* what the man had said on the telephone—several times. Because of his snooping into her past life, she'd been disposed to dislike the man, but when he arrived, she found that she couldn't.

He was much like West in looks, except his hair was dark where West's was lighter. He didn't smile as much and his eyes held that same lonesome look that she had once taken for icy remoteness in West's eyes.

"Have you been in touch with the adoption agency at all, Lesley?" he asked. "I mean, since you saw Valerie's letter?"

"Not even since the adoption."

Will went on, "I know you don't want to believe this, but I think it's someone from the agency. Your friends all know about Valerie, don't they?"

"Valerie, yes. My closest friends know about West, too."

''The agency knows that Valerie is dead,'' put in West. ''She left them some money.''

They both looked at him in astonishment.

''How in the world...''

''You didn't tell me that.''

''Sorry,'' West said ruefully. ''I just recalled when you mentioned the agency. Her lawyer alluded to the bequest when he delivered her letter to me. As you'll remember, Will, at that time I didn't even know which agency.''

''That information may help.'' Will ran a hand across the back of his neck. ''I have an appointment tomorrow with a couple who seem the most promising candidates for cooperating. I'm hoping that when I tell them about your situation, they'll give me names.''

''If they know the names,'' Lesley reminded him. ''I didn't recognize the voice on the phone, Will.'' She linked her fingers and leaned forward eagerly. ''Listen, I want to go with you.''

Will pondered for a minute, flipping through the pages of his notebook. ''Who was the caseworker for Dallas's adoption?'' he asked, as though she hadn't spoken.

''His name was John Conniers. He was a man in his late forties or early fifties, I think.'' She smiled. ''He looked a little like Santa Claus, white beard and mustache, white hair, ah...portly build. He was a dear man, always laughing. Everyone loved him. I want to go with you to see the couple,'' she repeated.

Will frowned. ''No one by the name of John Conniers is working there now.''

''He isn't?'' That surprised her. ''I can't imagine him leaving, but maybe he found a better job.'' She shrugged, switching topics without skipping a beat. ''The mother will probably open up to me faster than to you. She and I have been through a similar experience.'' And depending on what happens, we could both be deeply wounded, she added, but didn't voice the thought.

''I'll check on Conniers, but I don't remember the name from the employee list. I'll call you.''

West had stayed out of the conversation. Now he leaned forward. ''She's right, you know, Will. It began as her investigation. She has all the background at her fingertips. A woman would feel more comfortable talking to her.''

Will's frown darkened to a scowl. ''West, you know me. I do not work with females.'' He regarded her. ''Nothing personal, but with me it is an iron-clad rule.''

Lesley saw a determined glint in his eyes. ''I'm a journalist first,'' she said. ''Forget I'm also a female.''

Will raised a brow and looked her over thoroughly. Lesley forced herself to remain motionless under his inspection.

West laughed, interrupting the moment and earning himself a glare from both of them. ''Bend your rules, Will,'' he urged. ''If you don't she'll take off on her own, and I'll feel better if she's with you.''

Will slowly shook his head. ''Well—I don't know. I'll have to think about this.''

That was something. Lesley nodded. She hoped he would give the idea a fair hearing. ''I can live with that, but I would like your decision as soon as possible. I'll be at the station. Can you call me there?''

''West pays my salary. I'll call him,'' Will declared. ''He can let you know.''

Lesley and West sat quietly together in evening shadows drawn over the deck like a gauze curtain. West sipped a welcome glass of dark red Burgundy and sighed with satisfaction. His shirt was soaking wet.

After dinner he had offered—and she'd accepted—to bathe Dallas in his own bathroom and put him to bed. The experience was like an education in poaching an egg without breaking the yolk: delicate and slippery.

Lesley had bathed, too, at the same time, in the bath off the guest room. She would return to her early hours tomorrow morning. Her alarm was already set.

She was wearing a nightgown, a pale pink terry-cloth robe and slippers when she stepped into the bedroom. She found West standing over Dallas's bed, looking down at the sleeping child. The image of his loving expression lingered in her mind.

She watched a cardinal sweep by, close enough to the deck to display the bright red color of the male making his way to his nest for the night.

Dusk was a civilized time of day, an hour for relaxing, a time to gather strength for tomorrow. "I have to go to bed in a minute," Lesley said, feeling for the first time the weight of her *un*civilized schedule.

West avoided looking at her. He plucked at his shirt, pulling it away from his skin. He sighed. "I know."

The crickets sang their evening song; a car passed the far side of the complex; somewhere a door slammed.

"I'm sorry about your shirt. I should have warned you."

"It's cotton. It'll dry."

"Well...it's almost eight o'clock."

West drained his wineglass and placed it on the floor beside his chair as he rose. He took her hand and pulled her to her feet beside him. "I'll walk you home," he said with a half smile.

She hesitated. "Okay."

"No hanky-panky, I promise."

She was finding that simply holding hands, when it was with this man, was a marvelous thing to do. "None?" She gave a mock pout.

"Nope. Believe me, it will be harder on me than you. No pun intended."

She giggled, the sound surprising her—she was definitely not a giggler. Then she grew serious. "There's always the weekend," she suggested, knowing full well what she was saying.

His eyes cut to her, blazing, then were hooded. His fingers tightened on hers. "Yes, there's always the weekend."

Once—it seemed aeons ago—he had told her that they shouldn't use sex to solve the problems between them. But as far as she was concerned, those problems no longer existed. At least, not in their original form.

West wasn't going to sue for custody of Dallas, and she was not going to keep him from knowing his son. How their relationship would develop wasn't clear yet. But she trusted him to care for Dallas, to love him as much as she did.

Complete trust was another very big step for the defiant, aggressive child she had once been.

They reached her door and before she realized what was happening, West had backed her against the wall, his palms flat at her shoulder height. His mouth swooped down, covering her willing lips. That was the only place their bodies touched for a long, heart-stretching minute. Then his tongue thrust into her mouth, exploring.

Her response was powerful, visceral and totally un-planned. She seized the opportunity; she was aggressive. She met his tongue with her own in a moist, sensual dance and wrapped her arms tightly around his waist to pull him closer. His shirt was soaking her robe, but she didn't notice and wouldn't have cared if she had. This was reckless; this was heady.

His arousal was steel hard against her lower belly. Unconsciously, she arched her back to meet his hips.

He groaned and wrenched his mouth from hers. "Please, honey, don't move against me like that," he pleaded as he scattered hot kisses across her face.

She froze. "I—"

"For God's sake, don't say you're sorry," he grunted, cutting her off with another devouring, but brief, kiss. "You feel like heaven. It's the timing that's hell." His voice had dropped to a whisper.

He buried his face in a fistful of her sweet-smelling hair. His hungry lips found the delicate, delicious spot where neck and throat and ear meet. She shuddered as his mouth moved down to the opening of her robe where her flesh rose.

He cupped her breast, lifting her higher. Her skin was hot and flushed beneath his wandering lips. He groaned again and she felt the slide of his tongue. "I want you, Lesley."

Her fingers slid up to dig into his thick hair. "I want you, too." Was that her voice, deep with molasses-rich passion?

With a superhuman effort West put his hands on her shoulders to keep her where she was and stepped back. Though she leaned toward him, he held her away. "Please, honey," he appealed to her. "Unless you want to end up in my bed tonight."

She paused, thinking and letting the wall support her head. Her neck seemed incapable of bearing the weight. She tried to smile.

He chuckled and shook his head. "Not funny," he said. "When we make love for the first time, it is going to be perfect and complete. We won't have to keep one eye on the clock."

She nodded, swallowing hard.

His voice dropped an octave. "We'll take the whole night. I have this overwhelming urge to explore every inch of you."

Every inch? The comment made her pause. She was thirty-three years old. While she liked to think she was in good shape, what would West think of her body? Would he regard her as too skinny, too busty, too tall? Would she be embarrassed?

No. Her momentary doubt disappeared, blown away on a current of insight. She loved and trusted this man.

His own feelings were less clearly defined. She knew he wanted her. Suddenly, as she looked into his eyes, she became aware of an impressive trait, one that she hadn't recognized but that she greatly admired. West would never demoralize anyone.

He might not agree with her career plans; he might become angry, even furious; but he would not disparage her or anyone else on a personal level.

"Do we have a date?" he inquired. His eyes flashed watchfully.

"Yes, we do have a date. Definitely," she promised.

"Saturday, okay? I don't want you falling asleep on me."

He grinned, but she could see the effort it took.

"Not the first time anyway."

And she had to get up at three-thirty tomorrow morning. She knew he was right. She, too, wanted the first time to be as truly extraordinary as it promised to be.

Her mind rationalized that way; her heart was another matter. Her heart would have led her to his room tonight. "Okay," she said at last. She summoned a grin, activating the dimple. "They say anticipation is the largest part of the pleasure, or desire deffered is—"

West made an explosive sound deep in his throat. "I don't know who the hell *they* is, but they're out of their ever-lovin' skulls!"

The next afternoon Will came by to tell them that the woman who was his most promising prospect was traveling on business. "Her husband wouldn't talk unless she was present," he said in distaste. "By the way, Lesley, when the man called you, you did tell me everything he said, didn't you?"

Ad nauseum, thought Lesley. "Every word."

His brows rose. "And you didn't say anything?"

"I hung up on him."

He sighed his satisfaction, then he smiled. The sign of pleasure in his expression was such a rarity she was taken aback for a minute. "Good. If these people don't cooperate, maybe he'll try you again."

"Hey, now wait a minute, Will—" West put in.

But Lesley cut him off excitedly. "Right! I hadn't thought of that, either, but he could only reach me at work."

"And I always like to have an alternative plan," said Will. "Anyway, the man's wife will be home late tonight. We have an appointment with them at four tomorrow." He became fully serious again. "They live out of the city. We'll go in my car and I'll drive. I'll pick you up at eleven-thirty."

Lesley nodded. "I'll be ready. But, West, is that time okay with you?"

"It's fine. I'll take care of Dallas." He'd already made up his mind to wear out the child; he wasn't sure how, but he'd come up with something. He wanted Dallas to sleep like a rock Saturday night.

However, right now his thoughts were tuned in a different direction. "Will, I don't want Lesley and Dallas involved in a situation that might be dangerous."

Lesley glared at him. "Don't coddle me, West. You may coddle Dallas—he's a child. But I'm a grown woman. With a job to do."

West left for the office as soon as Will had gone. He laughed to himself as he drove.

Lesley had certainly put him in his place when she ordered him in no uncertain terms not to coddle her. He wanted to, he realized abruptly. He wanted to take care of her. That was a risky mentality for a man to have when dealing with a strong woman.

He'd have to practice being subtle.

Or maybe it wouldn't matter. She was a talented woman. How long would it be before the network would transfer her to a larger market?

By the time he parked his car, the remnants of his smile had disappeared completely.

Luke had been going over some paperwork he'd faxed in earlier. They finished up the work they had to discuss and Luke was about to leave, when West asked, "Could I talk to you for a minute?"

"Sure." Luke relaxed in his chair.

West used both hands to comb his hair back from his forehead. "She's driving me crazy, Luke!"

Luke grinned. "I presume you mean Lesley."

"God, yes! Her schedule, my schedule, Dallas—we can't seem to get together."

Luke steepled his fingers and hid his mouth. "And to what are you referring when you say 'get together'?"

"You know exactly what I'm talking about. She wears an old terry-cloth robe that makes her look lumpy. Dallas is a constant handful, so she's harassed and tired much of the time. And she's the sexiest woman I've ever seen in my entire life."

"I'm assuming that she feels the same way you do?" Luke asked after a minute.

West looked at his partner darkly. "Yeah."

"Are we talking just sexual attraction here, or something more committed?"

"I don't know. I realized I'm the one who started this. Clumsily, too. You gave me some good advice back then."

"Which you ignored."

"Yeah," West said. When he spoke again, he felt his way, thoughtfully, not certain what he wanted to say or how he wanted to say it.

"This all began as a yen—" he shook his head sharply "—no, as much more than that—a straightforward need to see my son. To see what he was like. To see if he was all right.

"Almost immediately, I was attracted to his mother, and now the attraction has built to desire that's spreading as fast as a California wildfire. And she's living at my place." He aimed a wry look at his partner. "At night, if I could reach through the wall behind my bed I could touch her.

"But there's more, Luke. My feeling for her is not solely a blaze of desire." He looked inward, contemplating. "Sometimes it's like sitting in front of a warm, comforting fireplace late at night, relaxing after just winning a big case. Happy. Content. Having the two of them there—it's almost as though we're a family." He rubbed his eyes with the heels of his hands and sighed. "That part of it is strange to me.

"So." He leaned forward, letting his hands dangle between his knees and went on, "I'm beginning to believe I want more from her. And I've got to ask myself what I can give in return. Am I worthy to be a husband and father? I've never had a sustained relationship of any kind before. Am I fooling myself?"

Luke answered reassuringly. "Oh, I think you're both worthy and capable of giving whatever you have to give. There's only one question that is appropriate here, West. Do you love her?"

West spread his hands. "How do I know? I like having her with me, and she sure as hell turns me on. I love Dallas—"

He broke off. "I do love him," he repeated wonderingly. He remembered his son's remark about Eunice: "Love is bigger than like." He told Luke about it and Luke's mouth turned up at the corners.

"That isn't enough where Lesley's concerned, and you know it."

"You mean, would I marry her only for the sake of having him? No. At least, I don't think so."

"Let me play devil's advocate." Luke paused. "This is no reflection on Lesley. I hope you understand that."

West nodded. He knew what was coming. "You can't ask anything that I haven't already asked myself."

Luke shrugged. "Then...would she marry you for the same reason? Under those conditions, there would be no question of a custody battle."

West got to his feet. He paced for a minute, ending at the window. He stood there, looking out.

But he wasn't seeing the trees or the buildings; he was seeing Lesley's face. At one time, he had wondered himself if she would enter into a relationship—hell, even marry him—solely to avoid a custody battle. Now he shook his head.

"I can't believe she would. She has acknowledged before witnesses that I'm his father. She didn't have to do that," he observed. "But there's also the matter of her career. What if she's transferred?"

Luke sighed and tilted his chair onto its back legs. "If I give you some advice, are you going to listen this time?"

West turned back. He crossed his arms and smiled, but his heart wasn't in it. "Maybe. If it's good advice."

Luke grinned back. "All my advice is good, you rat."

"Okay, shoot."

"We've got a client who's going to start a business in New Orleans."

West nodded. He knew the client; he knew New Orleans; he knew the maze of authorizations, licenses and permits that the man would have to traverse around that city's bureaucracy.

"One of us will have to spend some time—a week or ten days—down there," Luke continued. "If you go, it will give both of you some time and space to think about your feelings. Right now you're doing most of your deliberating with your gonads."

West was surprised by the offer. "I thought you wanted to handle that client. You were going to take Alex and David as soon as he got out of school for the summer, weren't you?"

"We can go another time. Besides, Alex would do anything for the cause."

"Cause?"

"She thinks you and Lesley are perfect for each other."

West felt the tension drain from him, tension he hadn't known was there. He laughed, easily, comfortably. The laughter relaxed the bunched muscles in his neck and across his shoulders.

The memory of some of Alex's blatant matchmaking attempts had him shaking his head in added amusement. "She says the same thing about every woman I speak to more than once."

"I know. It's a fact of life. Married women can't stand seeing an unattached man without wanting to do something about it."

Lesley was feeding Dallas his supper, when the telephone rang. She licked peanut butter off her fingers as she reached for it. "Hello?"

There was a pause on the other end of the line. Her heart gave a shocked leap of terror. Her initial thought was that the blackmailer had found them!

Then a voice, warm and cultured and very female, said, "Have I reached West Chadwick's residence?"

Oh, no. It must be one of his girlfriends. She should have let the machine take the call.

Annoyance and irritation quickly supplanted her chagrin. Her chin rose a notch.

West shouldn't be having girlfriend calls when his son was in his house, she rationalized. "Yes, it is," she informed the caller evenly. "This is a friend. West is out at the moment, but I'd be happy to take a message."

"Mommy, my san'wich is dripping jelly," said Dallas in the piercing voice he used when he was displeased.

Lesley held the receiver to her ear with her shoulder as she grabbed for paper towels.

There was another pause on the line, this one longer. At last the woman said, "This is West's mother. Would you ask him to call me, please?"

Her voice was just as warm, just as cultured as before. But overlaying those qualities was avid curiosity.

Lesley opened her mouth to identify herself to the woman she'd interviewed, then she shut it again. "Certainly," she said.

West came in late that night. He found Lesley asleep on the sofa. As he carried her to her bed, she made a soft, whispering sound and nestled against his chest. He flirted with the idea of veering to his own room, waking her in his own bed.

But he fought the temptation.

Lesley was the only woman he knew who could make him lose his usual control, control that had become such a part of him it was like another limb. He was not comfortable with the feeling.

He made his way into the kitchen, where the light still burned. There was a note prominently displayed against the coffeepot: "West, your mother called. She wants you to call her back. Love, L."

He groaned. Lord, his mother and father would give him fits when they found out he had a son—they had a grandson. Their first grandchild. Possibly their only grandchild.

He wandered back into the living room, dropped into a chair and stared at the note in his hand.

If only you'd been different, Mother; if only you'd showed me you cared about me more than business once in a while. If only you'd tossed a ball around with me occasionally, Father. If only you'd been there when I broke my arm, when I scored a touchdown, when I graduated. If only....

Those were the saddest, most pathetic words in the language. And the most futile.

At last, he looked at his watch. It was too late to call them tonight. He would call tomorrow. Maybe.

Maybe? If she didn't hear from him before lunchtime, she would just call back. Hell. He crumpled the note and tossed it overhand into a trash basket. Two points.

Before he turned off the light and went to bed himself, he looked in on Lesley and Dallas one more time. They were both sound asleep in the matching beds. Covers pulled across their shoulders, they had turned to face each other across the small gap that separated them.

He smiled to himself. He felt a glow of affinity somewhere in the region of his heart—they were here; they were safe.

Lesley opened her eyes to early sunshine. It was Saturday.

Her eyes sought and found Dallas in the other bed, lying on his side, his small fist curled under his cheek. She smiled sleepily and closed her eyes again.

When next she woke, the bed across from her was empty. She sat up abruptly, fear sending her heart on a rapid slide.

Then she remembered—she wasn't alone. She lay back, her cheek on the soft pillow, and curved her body into a ball of contentment.

West had Dallas. West was sharing her responsibilities for now. It felt good to have someone, curious but good. She missed Eunice; Eunice shared her commitment and took a lot of the burden from her.

But Eunice had other relatives, too. Most important she had a son who loved her. Granted, he was far away, but his love was always with her.

West was also sharing the joy of being a parent. After a shaky beginning, he took to it naturally. She smiled. She would have to watch him, or he would smother Dallas with concern for his safety.

She rolled to her back and stretched.

Tonight she shouldn't have to go to bed early. She wouldn't be tired.

Tonight.

The sensual tension stretched between them like the string of a tightly tuned guitar. His affectionate glances and molten gazes, the atmosphere of expectancy, had raised her level of desire to a point where she could hardly wait until tonight, no matter what followed.

It could have happened last night. The expectation, the stirring desire, had been there from the moment she'd walked in from work.

But West had had to go to his office to catch up on work he'd neglected while he tended his son in the mornings. He'd been delayed. By the time he'd come in she was sound asleep on the sofa.

He'd carried her to the room she shared with Dallas. The memory of his strong arms, his muscular chest beneath her cheek, was potent.

She wanted West desperately. And he wanted her. His body made that abundantly clear.

She stretched again and smiled again. She intended to wear her son out today; tonight he would sleep like—like a baby.

She glanced at the clock.

First she had an interview to do. She got out of bed and headed for the closet. What should she wear? She didn't want to be a too-formal on-air personality, but neither did she want to be so casual that she lost her credibility.

She dressed in cobalt-blue slacks and a man-tailored off-white shirt, which she softened with a tan-and-blue scarf tucked into the open neckline like an ascot. The slacks were belted in the same tan color. She brushed her hair vigorously. A touch of mascara and muted lipstick, and she was ready to go.

With Will. The stubborn man still hadn't revealed the name of the couple. He would be here at eleven-thirty. Surely he would tell her something then.

Or would he? He was an enigmatic man. West had said he'd trust Will with his life. But he also told her that Will did dislike working with women.

Too bad.

She left the room with a definite spring in her step.

"'Morning," West said with an unrestricted smile.

He sat beside Dallas in front of an almost empty bowl of cereal. Most of the milk had splashed onto the table and on Dallas's pajamas. West had a washcloth ready to clean him up.

"'Mornin', Mommy. I mean, Mom," Dallas greeted her. "You look pretty."

West gave her a quick inspection, head to toe. "Yes indeed." The appreciative expression in his eyes was full of promise.

She felt heat bloom in her cheeks. Clearly their thoughts flowed along parallel lines.

Lesley dropped a kiss on top of her son's head. "Good morning, sweetheart, thank you," she said. Her gaze however, lingered on West's smile. "Did you find the message from your mother?"

His smile faded. He lifted the child down and wiped his hands and face. "Yeah, I found it. I'll call her later."

"Dallas, go take off those wet pajamas," she told her son. "I've laid out your clothes on the bed."

"I can dress myself," the child proclaimed to West. He vanished into the hall.

West looked dubious, but Lesley reassured him. "He can do it. We might have to turn the shirt from back to front, but thank goodness for elastic and Velcro."

"I'm sorry Mother called. I hope she didn't upset you." What he really wanted to know was what Lesley had said, but he didn't ask.

"Not at all." Lesley laughed. She felt as light as eiderdown today. "No, West, I didn't tell her who I was," she teased.

West tossed the cloth into the bowl. "I didn't ask that," he protested, chuckling himself as he caught her wrist and pulled her onto his lap.

She linked her arms around his neck. "But you wanted to know."

"Not really." He nuzzled her ear. His broad palm swept up her back toward her nape.

She shivered with enjoyment. She was already leaning forward in anticipation of his thrilling kiss, when she suddenly thought of something. Placing two fingers in the center of his chest, she pulled her head back. "You probably ought to know before you speak to her... I'm sure she heard Dallas talking in the background."

His hand halted its progress. His face took on a rueful expression. "Then I'll have some explaining to do, won't I?"

It was Lesley's turn to want information, but she, too, was unable to ask.

"They're going to have to know sooner or later," he mused, surprising her.

"I told her I was a friend. I didn't explain the child's voice, either. Maybe she'll think it was television."

"She didn't recognize your voice?" He was surprised. His mother was usually quicker than that.

"Evidently not."

They were both wrong. Christine Chadwick had been on the phone to her friend Caroline Chandler early that morning.

Angie and Jesse Spears lived in a nice house in the suburbs. Will parked in the driveway and waved to Jesse, who was trimming the hedges with a wicked-looking pair of clippers. He returned the wave, but he didn't smile when he met them at the front door. He knocked twice with the back of his knuckles. The door opened immediately, as though at a prearranged signal.

Angie was young, probably in her early twenties. She was visibly nervous, but she also seemed to be determined. She showed them into the living room.

When they were all seated she took a deep breath and plunged right in; she even squeezed her eyes shut for a second, like an unseasoned beginner about to jump from the highest level of a diving platform. "Mr. McCarty, Jesse doesn't agree with me, but I've decided that I want to cooperate with you. I can't live under this pressure."

"We can move," said her husband.

She shook her head. "We've sent our daughter to stay with—"

"That doesn't matter to anyone except us," her husband interrupted harshly.

"No, of course not." She seemed to wilt slightly. "But I miss her terribly. And I don't want to move. My husband has a good job and so do I. Both our families live nearby.''

''We have the money,'' Jesse said.

''In our child's education fund. Mr. McCarty says that blackmailers don't stop. What will we do next time?''

''I'll get it somehow,'' he said moodily.

''Would you explain to Ms. MacDonald and me exactly what the man said?'' Will asked.

''He said that the birth mother had contacted him— she was having second thoughts. Recent rulings from some courts had stirred up her feelings. He also said that she couldn't decide whether to try to get her child back or to leave this part of the country and begin anew. She's leaning toward leaving.'' Angie's expression became cynical. ''But unfortunately the poor woman doesn't have enough money to move. He asked if I would be willing to contribute to a fund for her.''

''How horrible for you!'' whispered Lesley, unable, despite strong evidence to the contrary, to believe that anyone could be so heartless as to use a child as a pawn in this ugly game.

Angie smiled sadly and turned back to Will. ''When I asked him how he was involved, he said that he was acting as an intermediary. I pressed, but he wouldn't explain any more. In fact, the more I pushed, the more belligerent he became. That was when he said he would try to keep the woman from simply stealing the child.'' Her eyes filled with unshed tears. ''It was a threat—a clear threat—and it worked.'' With obvious effort, she contained herself before she went on.

''The man wants me to meet him Sunday night, with ten-thousand dollars in a paper sack. At a church, would you believe?'' Angie seemed outraged more by the location than about the money. She mentioned a church in downtown Atlanta; the congregation was probably very slim on Sunday nights. "I'm to be there for the seven o'clock service. I'll sit in the back pew, and when I leave I'll drop the sack on the floor."

Jesse seemed about to explode as he listened to his wife reveal the details of the delivery procedure. "Angie, are you crazy? These people—" Jesse broke off, indicating Lesley and Will.

Lesley intervened. "Did the two of you know that I've had a call, too?"

"McCarty mentioned it," said Jesse grudgingly.

Angie was surprised. "I didn't know that. But I do know one or two others, people we met at the agency, who were filling out forms or being interviewed, whom I called. They wouldn't give me permission to use their names." It was nearly an apology.

"I understand that. They feel susceptible and powerless," Lesley said.

"Does he want money from you, too, Ms. MacDonald?" Angie asked.

Lesley leaned forward earnestly. "My situation is a bit different. My child's birth mother died a few months ago. Clearly, the man didn't know that. Mr. McCarty thinks that the adoption agency is involved."

Angie thought for a minute, her brows furrowing. "I can see why you would think that," she said, surprising everyone except Will.

"But I don't. In fact, it couldn't be, because Valerie—she's the birth mother of my son—left a sum of money to the agency in gratitude. They *know* she died."

"Who was your caseworker?" Angie asked suddenly.

Lesley's feature's softened at her memory of the man. "John Conniers. He was very kind," she said. "Did you ever know him?"

"He was our caseworker, too. Did you know he retired last year?"

"No," muttered Lesley after a moment, beginning to put together the pieces. "Since he doesn't work there any longer, he might not know about Valerie's death or the money she left." She shook her head decisively. "But I just can't believe it of him. And I'd swear it wasn't John who called."

"No," agreed Angie. "I didn't recognize the voice as his, either. I guess that leaves us right back where we started."

"Not necessarily," Will observed. "He could have enlisted someone else to help him. If you'll let us follow you tomorrow night, Angie, we can see."

"I'm going with her," said Jesse.

"So am I," Lesley added.

Both the Spears looked unnerved at her declaration. Jesse started shaking his head.

"He might not like that," Angie said slowly.

"He wouldn't like it one damned bit," Jesse said.

"I'll stay out of sight. But this is really important to me. Not only for my little boy's sake—that is primary—but my reputation is on the line.

"I need to either clear the name of the agency or bring the authorities down on them. If I gave out incorrect information, I have to be the one to correct it. I hope you understand."

"Yes, I do understand, but how?" Angie smiled for the first time. "You're not exactly unrecognizable."

"Will can work something out. Can't you, Will? Get me there early. I might hide in the choir loft or something with a directional mike and a camcorder."

Will was silent. "I have to think about it."

Lesley knew she had won.

Chapter 11

Will McCarty pulled up in front of the condo but didn't kill the engine.

"Don't you want to come in? Shouldn't we make some plans?" Lesley asked, looking at him in the murky light left of the day. The halogen safety lamps that lined the oval were just beginning to come to life.

"No," he said bluntly, his rugged face giving nothing away.

She didn't know whether he meant "No, he simply wasn't coming in" or "No, she wasn't going to be in on the planning" or "No, she wasn't going with them tomorrow night." She was determined to wait for an excuse, her hand on the handle of the door.

"I have some thinking to do. I'll call later."

She presumed that was all she'd get. "Okay. Good-bye, Will."

He didn't answer.

A man of few words, Lesley thought, but she shrugged and got out of the car.

When she entered the condo, she was met by total silence. She walked softly down the hall, checking both bedrooms, but they were empty. She retraced her steps to the kitchen. On the counter were the remains of something edible; she couldn't quite identify it.

She walked through the dining area. The table had been haphazardly wiped. She continued to the living room and stopped dead in her tracks.

West was sprawled in his favorite chair.

Dallas was sprawled atop his broad chest. The top of his head was tucked under West's chin, and West's large hand covered the child's back protectively.

They breathed in synchronization, both sound asleep.

Dallas fell asleep when and where he wanted. Occasionally, when she put him to bed, he wasn't quite ready. He would sing to himself or talk to someone she couldn't see. But at the right moment, he simply lay down, closed his eyes and he was asleep. On the bed, on the floor, at the table, on the ground, on a chair, in his car seat—he was out like a light.

But not since he was a baby had he ever fallen asleep in anyone's arms.

Dallas liked his space, his independence.

Lesley put her fingers to her mouth and blinked. She felt a thickening in her throat; a warm hand squeezed her heart. She had never known such kinship as they shared quite naturally after a relatively short acquaintance.

At this moment she endured the ever-present memories of her lonely childhood. They were endurable. She was an adult now and she could handle them. Her hand dropped to her side and she took in a deep, quiet breath to calm herself and reclaim her resilience.

Her eyes gleamed at the sight of the large man and the small child. She yearned to be an artist, if only for a brief time, if only to capture this one touching scene of father and son on canvas. The tenderness, the affinity of these two who were so much alike, affected her profoundly, held her engrossed. She felt the tears wetting her face before she was even aware they were falling.

Suddenly West's eyes opened. His gray-blue gaze darkened, locking with hers.

Her tears ceased as though turned off by a valve. Her heartbeat quickened.

Slowly he smiled.

Dallas had awakened only long enough to brush his teeth, go to the bathroom and put on his pajamas.

West hovered, thinking the ritual took forever, but at last he was ready for bed.

As soon as he was tucked in, kissed good-night by both adults, he closed his eyes and slept.

West shook his head in wonder, but his worries were on the woman beside him. She'd refused to meet his eyes and she'd chattered on and on, filling him in on the couple, Angie and Jesse Spears, and her trip with Will. She was behaving as though she was uncommonly shy. And nervous.

They stood hip to hip at the door of the bedroom, watching Dallas sleep. The emotional intensity between them had built steadily all during Dallas's bedtime preparations. Now it was thick enough to slice.

West's arm was warm around her shoulders; hers, around his waist. But she held herself stiffly.

So ... here we are, Lesley thought wildly. What next? Her sexual experience was sketchy, inadequate for a woman of her age, she supposed. But her few sexual encounters had been disappointing. Instinctively she knew it would not be that way with West. Nevertheless her self-consciousness had resurfaced.

Lesley had no idea that, when she looked up at West, all her concerns were reflected in her expression, there for him to read. He experienced an overwhelming tenderness and a resolve not to hurt her.

Though she had worked diligently all her professional life, though she had been a woman in a male-dominated world, she was still vulnerable. There was an element of innocence remaining within her, like traces of confusion within the small child who had been shuffled from place to place, person to person.

"Lesley," he said in a quiet voice. "Will you come to bed with me? Will you let me make love to you?"

Lesley suspected that he seldom had to ask. Besides, they had agreed on this—date, if that's what it was—days ago. She wanted him; he wanted her. And he'd said the first time should be perfect.

The fact that he had asked, that he was giving her the final choice, made the moment that much sweeter. Her concerns faded; her eyes glowed. "Yes. Oh, yes," she whispered.

He kept her beneath his arm and they walked slowly to his room. He closed the door firmly behind them.

Yet the king-size bed, with its fluffy gray comforter, loomed large in her eyes. "West, I should tell you, I don't have a whole lot of experience."

A smile played at his lips, grew into a grin. He laughed softly. "Good," he said. "Shall I explain as we go along?"

A dry laugh escaped her, easing the moment, and she smiled, too. "I'm not *that* green. No, it's just that for so long my focus has been on—" She broke off, let her lids fall to shield her eyes, realizing what she'd been about to reveal. *My career.*

"Your life, making something of yourself," he corrected for her. There was no judgment in his voice, just tenderness. "I made a big mistake, Lesley, when I assumed you would let your career interfere with your love for your son."

He rubbed her upper arm with soft strokes. She laid her forehead against his chest. "And I made a mistake when I didn't recognize the pleasure—no, West, the joy—of involving you in the care of *our* son."

West felt a surge of emotion. Of acceptance. He let his head fall back, closing his eyes in immense relief.

"If I go too fast for you, please tell me," he insisted, keeping his voice deliberately calm. "I wouldn't hurt you for the world. Anything that makes you feel uneasy—"

She put her fingers over his lips, stopping the words. "Thank you, West." Her thanks were for more, much more, than his promise to go slowly. "I—" His warm breath against her head sealed any further words in her throat.

West dropped a kiss on her hair, her shining, sweet-smelling hair. His voice became a whisper at her ear. "I feel like I've waited an eternity to make love to you."

He took her other arm, wrapped it around his waist, too, and pulled her securely against him, thigh to thigh, warm breast to hard chest. She tilted her head back, looked up at him, waiting.

His mouth roamed over her face, touching down along her brows, her temple, her cheek; gentle, sweet, light kisses . . . under control.

Until she gave a soft moan and turned her head, hungrily seeking his mouth. She felt the hard muscles of his back flex under her hands, heard him take in a rasping breath, smelled his tangy male scent.

When his mouth finally covered her parted lips, when his demanding tongue swept inside her mouth, pursuing hers, first there was the heat, the seething, simmering heat, and then—suddenly, unexpectedly—the tempestuous storm that hit her, as though destiny itself decreed the exciting, impatient sensations that surged through her veins, along her nerve ends.

Electricity, like lightning, arced between them once again. Sparks crackled. Fireworks exploded. Why this man, this time? she marveled, her thoughts spinning like brilliant pinwheels.

She answered her own question. Because what she felt for him was a deeper, more profound emotion than she had ever known. Without hesitation, she gave herself up to the overpowering sensation, to the passionate response she hadn't known she was capable of feeling.

Convulsively, West grasped her tightly to him; his arms became steel coils. And she knew the storm had struck him, as well.

He lifted her as he held her, until her toes were dangling above the carpet. He carried her to the bed, sat, then fell back, still holding her, still kissing her. His hands roved over her back from her shoulders, to her hips, to her thighs and back up to tangle in her hair.

"Clothes." The single word burst from his mouth into hers as though he could say no more.

They rolled to their sides, skittered up onto the bed, mouths still clinging. They separated just far enough for her to work at the buttons of his shirt, for him to open hers. He discarded the scarf, tossing it aside to land in a shimmering heap on the floor. He started to tug at her belt.

In moments they were naked. They both paused, drinking in the sight of each other.

Lesley was slightly daunted by the size of him. But he was magnificently made. She touched his broad chest. His skin was warm. The light dusting of hair there thickened and turned silky as it arrowed toward and nested around his arousal. She was staring.

He was staring. Her skin was like satin, flawless. Her waist dipped enticingly, her breasts—oh, God—they were beautiful, the tight crowns an elegant dusky-rose color. The incredible femininity of her hips, the soft down between her thighs—she lay before him like a banquet upon which he was invited to feast. He couldn't breathe.

He caressed.

She stroked.

"Lesley, yes . . . there . . ." he moaned.

"You . . . that feels . . . oh, dear . . ." She sighed.

At last, he drew her into his arms again, molding her soft curves to his hard planes, as if he would merge their two bodies into one.

He moved atop her, balancing unsteadily to keep from crushing her. He kissed the lovely peak of one breast, then the other. His kisses quickened, grew more erotic; his tongue wet her; he suckled. He moved lower, nibbling, and she shuddered with excitement.

Then she felt his fingers tracing the sensitive skin of her inner thigh, to find the soft, wet heart of her desire. "Oh!"

Her gasp of pleasure almost sent West over the edge. Quickly he reached for the foil packet in the bedside table. He spread her thighs and nudged her with his swollen sex. He looked down into her lovely face. Her eyes were half-closed, but he could see the radiance of passion beneath her lashes.

He realized he was breathing like a marathoner. When he attempted to regain control over his own hunger, she made an earthy, provocative sound in the back of her throat.

"Yes, yes," she murmured urgently. "Now, please."

He tried to make himself go slowly, but the feel of her nails against his back, his hips, inflamed him more. The soft bite of her teeth at his shoulder—he was trembling with effort. He penetrated her soft, damp folds carefully but smoothly, unremittingly, until he was buried deep within her.

It was the most fantastic sensation. His head swam. She was tight around him as he began to move, so tight that he stopped for a moment, filling his lungs.

But her hips surged off the bed, silently demanding, provoking him to hasten his rhythm.

And he was lost.

Over and over he plunged into her, catching her soft cries of excitement with his mouth. She met him thrust for thrust.

She suddenly ceased to move; he heard her breath catch, hold. And then she fell apart in his arms, her body convulsing around his hardness in a throbbing, climactic spasm. Her sweet, trusting, total surrender touched his heart.

He released all restraint and fell with her into a void where there was no air, no light, just the miracle of intense, impassioned, torrid sensation.

A long time later, when he could breathe normally, when she could, he stirred, intending to roll to his side.

"No, stay here for a minute more," she said softly.

"I'm heavy," he warned.

"I'm strong," she countered.

"That you are, my heart."

Her eyes opened wide at the endearment. But his face was concealed in her neck; he didn't see her reaction.

He did, however, feel the contraction of the fingers that were tangled in his hair, hear her sweet sigh.

Without warning, his body reacted.

Good Lord! He was growing hard inside her. This was impossible, but the groggy haze that passed for lucidity told him otherwise.

West lay on his side, his face inches from Lesley's. She slept deeply. He studied every curve, every soft feature of her face, and smiled at the memories of the night. They had loved each other over and over and over.

He'd been spooked at first by his impatience and loss of control. He didn't *lose* control.

But—he grinned—he'd felt pleasantly punchy when he contemplated the miracle of his endurance. She was a spectacular and an inspiring woman. He couldn't get enough of her. And, it seemed, she of him.

As he watched, unaware of the tender smile on his face, a thin drift of dawn's illumination touched her hair where it tangled on his pillow. The tangle slowly became a smoldering ember.

A provocative sight.

It was almost dawn.

Dallas usually woke early.

Reluctantly, West eased his arm from beneath Lesley's shoulder and slid out of bed. He found a robe in the back of his closet and shrugged into it. The belt had long ago disappeared.

He returned to the bed, picked her up, sheet and all, and carried her to the twin bed in the other room. She didn't stir, except to roll to her stomach when he laid her down. He left a kiss on her shoulder.

Then he headed for the kitchen. Maybe a jolt of caffeine would clear his senses before either of them woke. Funny, it was usually he who had to be blasted out of bed.

Half an hour later, he stood at the window in a pair of jeans and nothing else, looking out as the world came slowly to life. He had just poured his second cup of coffee, when he felt her presence.

Lesley joined him at the window, knotting her own robe as she came to stand beside him. She touched his shoulder with her cheek. "Why did you move me?" she asked into the stillness.

He turned, smiled slightly and tucked her silky hair behind her ear. He handed her his cup of coffee—an intimate, reassuring gesture that she appreciated. She took a sip and handed it back. "Thank you."

"I thought we might avoid a barrel of questions if Dallas didn't find us in my room."

"You were right," she agreed ruefully. "He's licking his lips. That's a sure sign he's waking." She went to the cabinet and got herself a mug.

He watched her back as she poured coffee into the mug. What had he told Luke? That her bathrobe made her look lumpy. Not her waist—which was cinched by the tie. And not her bottom—which was smooth and rounded...and sweet. He remembered the feel of her in his palms.

"Lesley?"

She joined him again at the window and tilted her head up to meet his eyes. "Umm?"

He bent, kissed her with poignant tenderness. "Last night was very special," he murmured against her lips.

"To me, too, West." Her pulse stampeded the blood through her veins. She waited, wondering if he would say more.

Without warning, West's body reacted, rigidly. Damn! This was neither the time nor the place. He had no idea where they would go from here. He suspected she didn't, either.

He took a step back to gain some distance and regain control. At the counter, he topped off his coffee. "I talked to Luke yesterday," he said in a rush. "One of us has to go out of town, to New Orleans for a client, and it seems it will be me."

Lesley looked at him, hearing a roughness in his voice. The intimacy, the tenderness, had disappeared over the wide gulf that suddenly separated them.

Why? Did he think she was going to tie strings on him, on their lovemaking?

"When do you have to leave?" she asked evenly. What she wanted to do was throw herself into his arms and tell him how much she would miss him.

She was struck with a bizarre notion—had last night been an illusion? No, West couldn't have faked the passion they'd shared. But something had definitely changed this morning.

"I won't leave until Eunice gets back."

She barely remembered the questions he'd asked. Something was in the air—something dangerous, which hadn't been there before. Last night she would have sworn he had feelings for her, maybe even—no, she wouldn't count on love—but strong and definite feelings.

She fought off another idea—an unspeakable one— but it surfaced anyway. Had West decided to have a relationship with her to gain access to Dallas? Oddly, that cold-blooded logic had not occurred to her, not since the disastrous end to their first evening together.

She didn't believe it. But he did have a reputation around the city for always having an attractive woman on his arm. She knew he had the experience and she didn't; she probably wouldn't even *recognize* a seduction if it was planned carefully.

She shook her head once; she was being paranoid. She refused to think that West would do anything of a deliberately hurtful nature.

Since the day she and Dallas had come to stay with him, he hadn't mentioned letting the machine take his calls. And as far as she knew, no women had phoned except his mother.

Still, she didn't want him to get the idea that she was a clinging vine. "Nonsense," she said pragmatically. "You go today if your client needs you. I'll call the nanny service again and put some pressure on."

"Today is Sunday. You have an errand this evening, remember?"

The blackmailer. The church. Will.

And West had volunteered to keep Dallas. "Tomorrow, then. I can work something out."

Suddenly he was annoyed with her and he didn't know why. "Supermom can save the day?" He snapped out the question.

Her chin rose a notch. "If necessary. Besides, Eunice should be back anytime now. I spoke with her Friday. Her aunt is doing very well. If everything goes right tonight, Will can bring the police in. The Spears won't object after the blackmailer is caught. So there's no reason for me not to go home even if Eunice isn't there."

West was stunned by her sudden announcement. Who said anything about her leaving? He hadn't even thought that far ahead. Didn't want to. "No," he told her. "You and Dallas will stay here until Eunice gets back."

The familiar tilt of her chin was a warning he recognized. She opened her mouth to argue.

Fortunately, Dallas chose that moment to appear. "I'm hungry, Mom," he said.

Perhaps they could have found a moment during the day to sit down and thrash out their misunderstandings. But before an occasion presented itself, the situation between them began to deteriorate.

Things went from bad to worse; they exchanged barbs with chilly responses. Neither of them knew how to stop it.

West listened to Lesley explain to Dallas that he was going out of town. Tomorrow.

He said that she was mistaken.

She said that she couldn't be responsible for interfering in his business affairs.

He said that maybe she was just anxious to leave his home.

Eunice called, interrupting their too-civil exchange. "I'll be home tomorrow morning. Don't meet me—I'll take a cab. But can you leave a key somewhere at the house? I gave mine to West."

They worked out the details. "You don't know how happy I am. We've missed you," said Lesley brightly. "Dallas will be thrilled, too."

West left for his office soon after Eunice's call. "I'll phone my client and make my plane reservations for tomorrow," he said in parting. "Maybe we both need some space."

Lesley wanted to cry. The damned fool. Didn't he know she loved him?

She took Dallas to the park to swing. Then, after lunch, she sat staring into thin air while he had a short nap. Maybe West was right; maybe they did need some space; but she found that she hated the thought of leaving.

Will phoned to say he would pick her up at five. "I want you there early and well hidden."

She called Blanche and arrangements were made for sound equipment and a cameraman to be at the church well before five. At least this would soon be over.

West returned at four-thirty and found Lesley dressed in dark-blue jeans and a matching turtleneck. She had tied a navy blue scarf around her shoulders, explaining that she'd cover her hair with the silk square when the time came. Her sneakers were also navy.

"West is home," said Dallas, coming into the room as she arranged the scarf. "Gee, Mom, you look like, like—" He shook his head, unable to come up with a comparison. "A nighttime bluebird?" he finally finished lamely. "Are you going to sleep like that?"

"I'm going in late tomorrow, sweetheart, so I don't have to go to sleep early. But I have an errand to run tonight. West is going to take you out to eat."

West followed Dallas but stopped at the threshold of the open door.

She brushed past him.

"Wait." He handed her a cell phone and a card with a couple of numbers on it. "Stick this in your pocket." He eyed her backside. "If those jeans aren't too tight."

"I don't wear my clothes too tight," she answered huffily.

"Call me the minute this is over."

"Speaking of that, did you ever return your mother's call?"

He didn't answer.

"You should have, you know." She looked around for Dallas before continuing. He had gone back into the bedroom. "They aren't going to like it if they find out from someone else that they have a grandson."

He knew she was right. He knew the problems between him and his parents would have to be resolved—one way or another. And soon. He shoved his hands into the pockets of his jeans. "I know," he said, turning away.

When the doorbell rang at five o'clock, West waylaid her before she could answer. He pulled her roughly against him and covered her mouth with his before she could protest. "Be careful," he said harshly. "Do exactly what Will says." He kissed her again. "And don't take any damned fool chances."

Her heart pounded, her hope renewed. "N-no, I won't."

As soon as Lesley had left with Will, West grabbed his own cell phone and took Dallas to a local fast-food restaurant.

He ordered for them—a meal Lesley would hardly have approved. They found an empty booth, West sitting on one side, Dallas on his knees on the other. He had scoffed at the idea of a booster chair.

"What time will Mom be home?" he asked around a limp French fry.

"She will call us as soon as her business is finished," he told the child, patting the pocket of his jeans. "That's why I brought my flip-up." Flip-up was Dallas's nickname for the cellular phone.

The mention of the telephone reminded him that he had yet to return his mother's call. When the two of them were back in the car, he took the phone out of his pocket and punched in the number.

His mother and father had gone to the club for the evening, he was told by someone whose voice he didn't recognize.

He smiled and left a message. He'd done his duty.

West had just started the engine, when he had an idea. He checked the time. If he hurried he could make it.

"Dallas, how would you like to go visit with David for a while?"

"David! Yes, yes!"

Dallas was ecstatic when they reached the Quinlans' house on the river. He was welcomed warmly, as West had known he would be.

West borrowed a sport coat and a tie from Luke just in case. He arrived at the church at six-thirty. Before he could park and lock the car, Will was standing beside him.

"What the hell are you doing here?" he demanded. "You're crazy. I'm never working for you again."

"Why? No one knows me. The blackmailer has never seen me. He doesn't even know I exist."

If Will's stare had been loaded with bullets, he would be a dead man. "Look, Will, I can't stay out of this. Lesley and Dallas mean too much to me."

Will leaned against the car and looked at West. "I hate surprises," he said grudgingly, "but I guess you can stay in your car and keep an eye out."

"I could go into the church. I have a coat and tie."

"Absolutely not. Lesley is handling this like the professional she is. Can you imagine what would happen if she saw you in there? Hell, she'd fall apart and mess up the whole damned operation!"

She would? West thought that over and decided he liked the concept.

Lesley was well hidden. She was in the pastor's study, located to the left of the altar. With the door cracked she had a direct line of view up the side aisle.

The cameraman was also well hidden. He was in the dark balcony above the back pew where the Spears had been instructed to sit. At some point he would have to stand and point his camera down. By then, however, the congregation would be facing forward toward the altar. The directional microphone had been set in place, but she could see neither it nor the camera.

The choir loft had been ruled out. It was behind the altar and too far away from the scene of the action. A shame, because it was darkened. On Sunday evenings, the pastor had explained, the music was provided by a piano. It was out of sight below the balcony.

Will had prepared the man and sworn him to secrecy. The pastor had been cooperative but wary of Will's forbidding demeanor.

Will was outside. He would take up his position in the vestibule after everyone was seated. She was to signal him by opening the study door fully when she saw the man pick up the paper sack and start to leave. Will would detain him; the Spears would call the police. They would have the whole thing on film.

Her adrenaline was pumping. This was going to be one terrific story.

She kept her eyes fixed on the spot where the Spears had been instructed to sit.

Now all they had to do was wait.

* * *

Angie's hands were shaking as they entered; she clutched the neatly folded paper bag to her breast. Jesse was stone-faced. They entered the sanctuary and sat in the back row, as directed. No one joined them.

In the shadows beneath the balcony, unseen hands began to play soft music as the sparse crowd filed into the pews.

The pastor began the service. Still no one sat near the Spears.

Jesse put his arm along the back of the pew. He gave Angie's shoulder a squeeze, then he gripped the top of the wooden pew. Hard.

So hard that his knuckles were white.

Where was the man?

Outside, West waited. He had slid down in his seat so his head wouldn't show over the back. He watched as people arrived and entered the small church. Through his open window he could hear their chatter, but not their words.

No one looked sinister, he thought.

He chided himself—as a lawyer, he should know better than to stereotype. He peered at his watch under the faint light of a streetlamp almost a block away.

Seven-oh-five.

He sighed and wiped his palms on his jeans. Seventwenty.

Seven-forty.

Long-winded preacher. Seven fifty-five.

An engine purred to life and idled. He looked for the source of the sound.

A car was parked on the side street near the back of the church, about fifty yards away from the main thoroughfare. No headlights or taillights came on.

The doors to the church were still closed. West frowned.

Inside, the final hymn had been sung; the pastor pronounced the benediction and strode up the center aisle to be at the door when his parishioners left.

People began to stand, exchanging greetings with one another. They moved slowly down the aisles toward the vestibule, saying goodbye to the pastor. At last, Angie and Jesse, who had been dawdling, had to leave their ten-thousand dollars under the seat and walk out.

Lesley was devastated; she pounded her fist on her knee in frustration. No one had come near the young couple. The sanctuary was almost empty.

Suddenly, through the crack in the door, she saw the pianist coming down the aisle toward her. He was sauntering as though haste was the last thing on his mind. All the rest of the team was at the back of the church. She was alone here.

And the pianist held a neatly folded paper bag.

Chapter 12

Keeping his peripheral vision on the idling car, West watched as the doors swung back and people began to leave the church. It was a few minutes after eight o'clock and night had fallen with a vengeance. Without street-lamps the area would be pitch-black.

His gaze swept the area carefully, checking for a glimpse of Lesley or Will. The sky was overcast; if there was a moon he couldn't see it. A rainstorm, common in Atlanta in the spring, would put a final cap on this gloomy setting. And, if he wasn't mistaken, complicate Will's plans thoroughly.

Suddenly a figure darted from the back of the church, heading toward the idling car. Another figure followed closely, if furtively, behind.

West would have known the second figure anywhere.

He was out of his car and sprinting toward them in an instant. "Lesley, no!" he cried as he saw her grab the man's jacket and try to hold on. His heart pounding, he accelerated. "Lesley!"

And he saw the man turn on her, backhanding her with a powerful blow. She fell to the sidewalk—he could hear her head hit the concrete. And then she was still.

God, please God, he prayed. *Please let her be all right.* "Lesley!" he cried for the third time. He reached her and fell to his knees. He touched her lightly, but he was afraid to move her, afraid to do what he wanted to do—gather her in his arms and hold on to her. Forever.

He was only vaguely aware of what was going on around him. People yelling, running.

Will streaked past them, calling out, and two more men appeared, dressed in dark clothes. One grabbed the man who had hit Lesley just as he got the car door open. In seconds he was on the ground and handcuffed.

The other man went for the driver's side, jerked open the door and pulled out . . . Santa Claus!

"Call 911! Ambulance!" he shouted, forgetting the phone in his pocket and the one in hers. "Police, too," he added as an afterthought. He didn't give a damn what happened to the blackmailers. At this point all he was concerned about was Lesley.

She was inert, lifeless; she could be seriously injured. He could only grasp her hand, stroke her hair and murmur to her.

A man about to get in his car turned and hurried back into the building. "I'll call," the man cried.

The pastor joined West and took Lesley's other hand. "I've already called," he told West.

"Here, here, my man," said John Conniers as one of Will's associates put handcuffs on him, too. "What do you think you're doing?"

West chafed the cold hand he held. "Where the hell—sorry, Padre—is that ambulance?" he yelled to the church-dressed crowd that had begun to gather. Parishioners who had left, heard the commotion and were returning.

The pastor pointed to a woman who was running toward them. "Marianne!" he called. "Mrs. Link is a nurse," he told West.

From somewhere a bright light hit the scene and he could see the bruise that had begun to color one side of Lesley's face. His heart plummeted.

The woman took the pastor's place, placed her fingers at a spot on Lesley's wrist. "Her pulse is steady," she said.

Mrs. Link lifted one of Lesley's eyelids.

And the other one popped open. Lesley squinted at the strange woman. "Ouch. The light," she whimpered.

"Kill that light!" West yelled.

Her gaze swung to West. She inhaled fearfully. "Where's Dallas?" she demanded.

Before he could answer she said, "Hold me." She reached for him.

He held her, despite the sob in her voice, despite the disapproving look the nurse gave him. He raised her gently in his arms to a sitting position and cradled her warmly, tenderly, as though she might shatter. "Dallas is with Luke, Alex and David. Just be calm, honey. An ambulance is on its way."

"My head hurts!" She placed a hand over the spot where she'd hit the sidewalk; there was a knot there, but no blood on her fingers when she looked. Then she touched her face; it felt as if it had been burned with a hot iron. "I don't need an ambulance. What happened?"

Will spoke from behind West. "You tried to take on the blackmailers single-handed, you idiot," he said without a smidgen of sympathy. "Did you really think I'd leave the back of the building unguarded? Women!" He added the last word with disgust.

West was holding her now, his arms strong and secure, making her feel safe.

But Will had made her angry. "You're the idiot," she said as heatedly as she could manage when her head felt as though it would burst. "The strong, silent type. If I had known what your plans were I wouldn't have run after him. But no-o-o." She strung the word out. "You always have some 'thinking to do.' Ouch, you make my head hurt worse." She sniffed.

"You aren't crying, are you?" Will asked in horror.

"I wouldn't give you the satisfaction." She held her hand out to him. "Help me up."

"No!" said Will and West in unison.

"Yes," she said. But it was West who helped her stand, who held on to her when she made him take her to John Conniers. Her cameraman followed.

The police and the ambulance arrived at the same time. But Lesley was on camera.

At first Conniers pleaded ignorance. He was waiting there to pick up his nephew after church. At last, however, both men confessed to the blackmailing scheme. Fortunately for their victims, they had not spent the money they'd already collected.

John Conniers had been the brains behind the idea. The adoption agency was not responsible for any of their actions. All the adoptions were legal. John had copied the files before he retired, a goodly number of them, but he was too recognizable to their victims. So he had enlisted the help of his nephew, who played the piano and organ in this church. Who would suspect him?

The men admitted that they didn't plan to repeat their demands, which they kept fairly modest. Conniers had judged from the files what the victims could afford to pay.

"You're all heart," muttered Will.

Nor had they planned to spend any of the money until they could move from the area. They might have gotten away with their scheme had it not been for the erroneous call to Lesley.

The Spears were the fifth couple they'd approached. Lesley was to have been the sixth victim. When she'd hung up on them without responding in fear as the others had, they'd begun to have second thoughts.

Lesley went with the ambulance attendants to the hospital to be checked out, but not before she had taped her stand-up for the eleven o'clock news story.

Banged head, blackening eye and swelling cheek notwithstanding, West thought she was terrific.

Over Lesley's weak protests, the doctor insisted on keeping her overnight. "Merely as a precaution," he assured both her and West. "You'll be out of here in time for the noon show."

"What time?" she asked warily.

"I start morning rounds at seven. Another X ray, a reflex test. Say eight-thirty or nine?"

"I'd rather sleep at home," she said plaintively, pleadingly, turning her beautiful midnight-blue eyes on the doctor.

Her act didn't fool West, who stood against the wall, arms folded. He'd seen her in action before the camera. "Honey, you may as well stay," he said.

He was trying to keep his churning emotions hidden. In the bright light of the emergency room her swollen face was turning darker every minute. "I doubt that even your miracle makeup man will be able to hide that shiner by noon tomorrow."

Lesley hadn't thought about that. Or her son's reaction to her looks. "Dallas! He'll be so upset. Will you explain to him before he sees me?"

"Sure."

West had called Luke, to be told that Dallas was happily sleeping in the spare bed in David's room. West could pick him up in the morning.

"If he fell asleep without Hop, he should be able to understand." He told Lesley about the call to Luke. They shared a smile.

The doctor looked at them blankly.

"Don't ask," West cautioned the man.

When the doctor left to make arrangements for her room, Lesley turned to West. "I want to thank you for not trying to stop me from doing the story."

His mouth turned up at one corner. His eyes were warm and intimate. "I seem to remember being told not to coddle you."

"You could hold me again. That wouldn't be coddling."

He levered himself away from the wall and was across the cubicle before she finished speaking.

"Oh, West..." she said as his arms came around her, holding her tightly to him. There was no gentleness, no tenderness in him now, just fear and the need to know she was there, she was real, she was all right. He was actually shaking as he buried his face against her neck.

"When he hit you and you fell—"

The words were muffled, but she heard. "Shh." She gripped his shirt and held on. "I'm fine now."

"I heard your head crack when you hit the sidewalk. Do you know what that sound did to me?" he whispered brokenly.

She cupped his face and brought it up to hers, just the way Dallas did when he wanted someone's attention. She was shocked to see that his eyes were moist. "West, I love you," she said.

He kissed her briefly. Then he took her hand and held it firmly next to his beating heart. He started to speak. "Lesley, honey—"

Two nurses entered briskly at that moment, one wheeling a chair to take her to her room. "Ready to go?" asked the other. Neither of them was disposed to argue with these formidable women, but they both did laugh, communicating without words.

"I'll see you in the morning," she said when she was seated.

"And I'll be here as early as they'll let me in."

Their fingers parted reluctantly.

Dallas wrapped his arms around West's neck and cried brokenheartedly when West told him that his mother had been hurt. West could have wept himself as he held his son tightly to him.

David and Alex stood nearby. Alex dabbed at her eyes with a wrinkled scrap of tissue. She had offered to drive Dallas home herself, but West had vetoed the idea. "I promised Lesley," he said simply.

West rubbed Dallas's back, murmuring reassuring words. "Mommy had a bump on her head, but she'll be home today and in a few days she'll feel fine again, sweetheart," he said, using Lesley's pet name for the child. "Newness is waiting for you at home."

"And Mommy?" He glanced over at David. "Mom?"

"Your mom will be there, too—" West thought for a minute. Soon was an inadequate timeline for a child. "Before lunch. You've already had breakfast. What comes next?"

Dallas's sobs were diminishing. He raised his watery sky-blue eyes to West. His little brows were arched in fear. "Lunch," he said on a sob.

"That's right." He tried to smile. "Your mom will be there before lunch."

David came over and hunkered down beside them. "You know, Dallas, when I was three I said 'Mommy,' too."

"You did? You're not jus' sayin' that?"

David grinned and placed his hand over his heart. "Would your old truckin' buddy lie to you?"

Dallas relaxed in West's arms. "No," he said.

"Let's go home," West said.

Dallas nodded, hiccuping. "Bye, David, Alex. Come see me. You can bring Mr. Luke, too."

When West finally carried Lesley into her house, Dallas had been waiting at the door. His mouth dropped open. "Mommy, you look like—"

West gave him a warning look.

He sat her in a chair and her son climbed on her lap. She held him to her tightly, trying to smile, while tears formed in her eyes. "I know—I look awful right now.

But I'm so glad to see you. Did you have fun at David's?" Her smile was crooked.

"Yes." He cradled her face, very careful on the bruised side. "But I was sad that you got hurt. I turned your bed down. And I'll be real quiet unless you want me to read to you."

"Quiet? That'll be the day," said Eunice, bending to hug Lesley warmly.

"Did you say you turned back my bed, sweetheart? I don't know what was in my oatmeal this morning, but I'm sleepy."

Using the table for leverage, she got to her feet.

"You prob'ly had med'cine, too. Wes', you carry her," Dallas commanded. "She's wobbling."

West picked her up again. He felt her wilt against him, and realized what an effort it had taken to put on a good act for Dallas. He carried her to her bed.

Her normally shining auburn hair was slightly dulled from her ordeal. The strands spread on the pillow and her eyelids drooped as he laid her down. He knelt on one knee beside the bed and took her hand. "Honey, before you go to sleep, I need to tell you something."

"'Kay."

He kissed her knuckles. "I have to go to New Orleans this afternoon."

She frowned in confusion. "Why?"

"Don't you remember? You told me to," he said, smiling. "The day before. We had one of our disagreements. You told me not to keep my client waiting."

"I guess I was snappish," she admitted.

"Must be the red hair."

"My hair isn't red," she answered automatically, slurring her words. "It's—"

"I know. It's auburn. And it's beautiful, one of the first things I noticed about you. I'll be home as soon as I can."

Her eyes closed.

"Wait, Lesley, wake up for just a minute more."

" 'Kay." She cracked her eyes again.

"My mother and father saw us on television last night. She called me. They've promised not to bother you until you're better, but they know about Dallas."

She smiled blissfully.

West opened her hand. He closed his own eyes and placed a kiss on her palm. "Hold on to that kiss, my darling, until I get back," he whispered against her skin. "I love you, Lesley. You and I and Dallas are going to be a family."

When she made no response, he raised his head.

She was sound asleep. He kissed her soft lips, but she didn't stir.

"I think she should take it easy for a day or two, but I didn't tell her that," said West to Eunice a little later. "I don't think the doctor dared tell her, either." He grinned.

"He gave her something for the pain. She objected and he threatened to keep her there if she didn't take it. That's why she's so groggy. She may need another pill tomorrow, but after that, aspirin should be enough."

Eunice nodded. They stood at the kitchen window, watching Dallas shovel sand in the fenced play area. "She's always said her head is the hardest part of her."

"I agree with her. And thank God for it." He grew sober. "Listen, Eunice, if you need anything, please feel free to call Luke or Alex. I've left their numbers." He pointed to the message center on the refrigerator.

"I will, and thank you, West," she said warmly.

She seemed to have done an about-face in her opinion of him. He liked it. "I think that's everything. I've warned you about my parents, you have the name of the hotel where I'll be staying and I'll call tonight."

"Have you packed?"

"Lord, no! I forgot." He ran a hand through his rumpled hair and grabbed for his keys. "And my plane leaves at five."

Eunice walked with him to the door. "I had something I wanted to ask you, Eunice," he said hesitantly, rubbing the back of his neck.

"Certainly, West. If I can help I will."

"I need to know if you think I've bonded with them," he said as he opened the door. "Lesley mentioned bonding. It seems to mean a lot to her."

He saw her blank look. Misunderstanding, he added, "I know it's complicated."

"It isn't complicated at all, West. It means loving deeply, not only romantically but affectionately, too, and caring, being devoted. Yes, I'd say you have probably bonded with both of them."

Lesley woke to total confusion. The room was dark except for a narrow crack of light from the door.

She could hear someone whispering. "I'm awake," she said hoarsely.

The door opened fully. It was Dallas, Blanche, Abe and Eunice.

"Mommy!" Dallas ran for the bed. She knew what would happen when he reached it. He would jump and pounce on her. It was a game they played. Her part was to tickle him.

She put both hands to her aching head.

Dallas screeched to a stop, looking worried.

She forced herself to smile. "Sweetheart, may I have a gentle hug, instead?"

His expression cleared. "Okay." Moving slowly, he climbed onto the bed and hugged her. He stayed under her arm when she spoke to the others.

"Well, what do you think?" she asked.

Eunice had opened the drapes, but the sheer curtains beneath them remained closed, leaving the room softly illuminated.

Blanche came closer to the bed. "I hope that shiner clears up before the Peabody Awards."

"What?"

"Yep," said Abe. "The story went nationwide overnight. It has everything—poignance, sympathy, crime, violence and kids."

Her eyes widened. "Really?" she asked, her headache beginning to ease.

"Really," Blanche affirmed. She smiled, but there was a certain amount of distress in her voice. "They've already called from New York. They want to talk to you."

"This late?"

"Late," Eunice put in. "Today is tomorrow. You slept around the clock."

"The show!"

"I did the morning news and we put on a rerun for 'Lunch,'" said Abe. He grinned, too. "With a proper and serious announcement, of course. Our star is hospitalized."

"One of them," Lesley corrected.

Abe shrugged. "I'm not the jealous type. And you're the one with all the ambition. Anyway, it will probably be the best watched rerun in history."

When her co-workers had gone, Lesley asked, "Have you heard from West? I thought he would come by."

"Don't you 'member, Mommy? Wes' had to go on a plane to New Or-leans."

Lesley's brows drew together. "I'd forgotten. He told me, but I was so sleepy and...he said something else, too. What was it?" She put her fingers to her temple.

"Do you need an aspirin?" Eunice asked, making a face behind Dallas's back.

"What?" Then she got the message. "Oh, yes, aspirin would help. Sweetheart, would you bring me a glass of water from the kitchen?"

"You have a whole glass of water," Dallas reminded her. "On your table."

"But I'd like fresh water." She smiled. "Please."

"Okay." He left.

"Don't fill the glass too full," cautioned Eunice. She reached into her pocket and took out a handful of tiny envelopes. "A lot of flowers have arrived, but you might be especially interested in one arrangement...the Chadwicks'," she said, giving the cards to Lesley. "They not only sent flowers, they also called. I put them off, but I guess you'll eventually have to talk to them."

"Yes," Lesley said, sighing deeply. "That was what I'd forgotten."

West had told his parents about Dallas. She knew a moment's fear.

The Chadwicks were powerful people. She hoped he could finish his business in New Orleans quickly.

West had had it up to the wazoo with the damned bureaucrats. They were driving him crazy!

He was patient the first day as he went from one office to the next. To obtain one license, his client needed another permit, which could only be issued if he had another license. The afternoon of the second day, his client looked as frustrated as West felt.

Finally, the two men walked into an office for an appointment that was supposed to have taken place two hours ago. But as the man's secretary kept reminding them, he was very important and very busy.

West's client sat before the man's desk, but West remained standing. He shoved his hands into the pockets of his trousers and rocked on his heels. "Did you see the story on television about the newswoman who was injured in Atlanta?" he asked the man.

The man was surprised. "Yes, yes, terrible thing. Do you know her?"

"I know her very well indeed. She's the mother of my son. As you can imagine, I am very impatient to get back to them. The people you have working here are as slow as molasses in January."

The man huffed. He was not accustomed to being spoken to in such a manner.

But his wife thought that cute little redhead was wonderful. And she *was* with the press. He decided not to argue.

"Leave me your paperwork. It will be ready for you by noon tomorrow," he said.

West stood at the battered fence, his face like a study in chiseled stone. When he'd approached the park, looking for Lesley and Dallas, he'd had a hell of a shock, and he didn't know how he felt about it.

His heartbeat echoed hollowly within his chest, bringing forth unfamiliar feelings. Until he'd met Lesley MacDonald, he'd not been a man inclined toward gut-wrenching emotion, but she and her son had changed him.

As he watched the scene, discomfort warred with confusion, regret and—he had to admit—a certain pride.

He closed his eyes for a second and just as quickly opened them. The children's playground was again a medley of colorful activity and the serenity of the setting was in direct conflict with his own feelings once more.

Before him, on the other side of the fence, Dallas, with high-pitched laughter and gleeful giggles, celebrated a sunny day with joyous abandon.

The child's mother stood off to the side, watching fondly as Dallas ran in circles around Harold Westmoreland Chadwick II. Christine Chadwick sat near them, one sneaker-clad toe moving the swing in which she sat, back and forth in a slow arc.

West's hands curled in a tight grip around the top bar of the fence. A sense of destiny intruded somewhere near his heart.

Lesley saw him first. She spoke to Christine in a low tone and started toward the gate.

By the time they reached each other they were moving faster. West opened his arms and she ran into them. He closed them around her. "I love you," he said.

"And I love you," she answered. Their lips sealed the declaration hungrily.

Finally they broke off the kiss but continued to hold each other. "The last time I saw you…God, Lesley, I've missed you," he muttered, cupping her face, looking at every feature as though he could never get enough of the sight. "You still have a black eye." He pulled her back in his arms. "What are they doing here?" he asked over her head.

She ignored that question for now. "I've missed you, too. Luke said you would be gone at least a week. But three days is a record for New Orleans." Her smile was irresistible.

"I had a powerful incentive." He grinned down into her querying gaze. "I asked you to marry me, and you never answered." He linked his hands behind her back. "Do you remember?"

"I wouldn't have forgotten that," she said, shaking her head firmly. "No, I wanted it too badly."

"You wanted me to propose?"

"I've loved you for so long. The answer is yes. Yes, yes."

He kissed her again, this one long and serious and breath stealing. His voice was husky when he went on. "I told you the day I left for New Orleans that I love you." He paused. "You were snoring at the time."

"I don't snore," she said.

"Well, maybe not really snoring," he conceded. "More like a snuffling sound. Or maybe a—"

"West Chadwick—"

"We're arguing again." He gave a sigh and turned her under his arm. They headed back to the playground. "I guess it's the red hair. I never thought I'd marry a red-head."

"My hair is not red."

"I know." He chuckled. "It's auburn." He stopped and cradled her head gently. "Whatever, it's beautiful. You're beautiful."

"My hair is really mousy brown," she told him with a smug smile. "The auburn rinse looks better on camera."

For once he was speechless.

Dallas spotted them at that minute. He set off at a run. "Wes', you're home!" he yelled. "Mommy, you should have told me."

"So, do you want to take back your proposal?" Lesley asked before Dallas had reached the halfway point. "I know being married to a mousy-brown-haired woman would ruin your image. But you'd better hurry. I've decided that Atlanta is a large enough city for my journalistic goals and I want a big family, and we'll have to finish redoing the house, eventually add on. Once Dallas finds out—"

His kiss shut her up. "Now, about my parents . . . ?"

That evening, curled up in his arms on the sofa, she finally had time to explain. "They really regret the past, West. They told me about how often they left you on your own—more, actually, than you had told me. They don't want to make any more mistakes. They want a chance to get to know you again. Dallas, too. But you most of all. They've invited us for dinner tomorrow night."

"Do you like them?" he asked evenly.

"Yes, I think I do," she said, slowly, consideringly. "And they are Dallas's grandparents."

"Then we'll go to dinner. And see what develops from there."

They dined alfresco, on the Chadwicks' terrace overlooking a wide expanse of lawn bordered by rosebushes. Caroline had said to dress casually. To West that meant jeans.

Lesley wore a sundress; Dallas, a new playsuit.

The evening was less strained than West had expected it to be. Mostly because of Dallas.

The child was slightly awed at first by the size of the house and was content to stay on West's lap.

But it didn't take long before he was running in and out of the house. In a very short while, he knew all the servants' names and the names of their children.

Finally, he broke the last barrier. "Wes'," he said, tilting his head and looking innocent.

West hid a smile, wondering what was coming. He reached for Lesley's hand under the table. "Yes, Dallas?"

"I call Mommy 'Mommy.' Or sometimes 'Mom,' like David. And you said I could call you 'Dad' because we're getting married."

Then he waved his hand in a grand sweep toward Christine and Harold. "Why do you call them 'Mother' and 'Father'? It sounds...funny. Don't you like 'Mom' and 'Dad' for names?"

"Well..." West didn't know how to answer. Lesley squeezed his hand reassuringly.

Suddenly Harold said, "You're right, Dallas. It does sound funny." He seemed to be holding his breath as he looked at his son.

Christine spoke up. "I personally like it—them. I mean any—"

"I think we know what you mean...Mom," said West.

Epilogue

Thanksgiving had always been Lesley's favorite holiday, but her memories of the occasion as a child and young adult were bittersweet.

This Thanksgiving was different—joyous, unlike any other she'd ever spent. She looked around, feeling a warm heart and a genuine thankfulness, her eyes misty as they touched each member of the family and each of the friends around her.

Luke and Alexandra were seated across the table with David. She and Alex had become close during these past weeks. She herself sat in one of the high-backed upholstered chairs between West and Dallas. Eunice sat on the child's other side. At the head of the table was West's father, and his mother was at the other end.

She and West had been married for two months. She had quickly gotten over her awe of his parents, and the atmosphere was beginning to thaw among all of them.

They could thank Dallas for the relaxed ambience. His newly found grandparents sincerely doted on him. They occasionally needed interpretation from either West, Eunice or her, but they were learning that he had definite ideas of his own. After several visits he had become quickly at home in the large house.

She smiled to herself. Yesterday she had dropped by to see if she could be of any help. Not that she had really expected to be taken up on her offer, but she'd been in the area. Dallas had taken one look at the splendidly set dining-room table, with heavy cut glass and shining silver candelabra, and his small face fell. He shook his head.

"Christine, that isn't the way the table is supposed to look. I saw in my Thanksgiving book. The plates and forks and things are okay," he'd said, dismissing fine Meissen china and the elegant old silver with a word. "But you're 'posed to have fruits and vegetables in the middle, in a pointy basket."

"A pointy basket," Christine had replied, nodding.

Lesley held her breath, wondering if her mother-in-law would take offense. But she relaxed when Christine replied.

"Of course. What on earth was I thinking? On Thanksgiving we must have a cornucopia. That's the pointy basket," she explained as she reached for the candelabra and handed them to the butler, who placed them on a sideboard. "I promise we'll find one and fill it with something appropriate. Perhaps you could let me see your book so I'll be certain to get it just right."

"It's in the car. I'll let you borrow it."

Lesley started to protest his leaving alone; but the butler, of whom Dallas had already made a friend, signaled that he would accompany the child.

Since yesterday the table had undergone a startling transformation. The brightly colored apples, oranges, peppers, squash, corn and nuts of all kinds were a wonderful contrast to the white table linens. There were also candles, several of them, but they were in short, brass candlesticks. The cornucopia itself was fashioned of natural wicker, like a basket.

The golden turkey in all its glory was before Harold's plate. He held the carving set masterfully. There were a least ten other dishes, from cranberry sauce to sweet potatoes in carved orange baskets. A scrap of a quotation about a "groaning table" occurred to her.

When they'd entered the dining room, West had blinked at the sight, but she'd squeezed his hand, hoping he wouldn't comment. He squeezed back and leaned down to whisper, "We usually have stuffed pheasant and wild rice, and it's all served from the kitchen."

She grinned.

He complimented his mother on the arrangement, earning himself a genuine smile. "It's from Dallas's book," she explained, smiling down at her grandson. "He let me borrow it."

"You've added some stuff, Christine, but I guess it's okay," proclaimed Dallas. "As long as we have pumpkin pie."

"Oh, yes," she assured him.

Lesley's smile faded. Her son's use of his grandmother's first name reminded her that she and West had agreed to tell Dallas the truth today. Today he would find out that he was actually West's son, and Christine and Harold's grandson.

He had asked West if he could call him "Daddy" as soon as their small wedding was over, and now he easily accepted West's presence in their home.

But she had absolutely no idea how he would respond to the whole truth.

"Uh-oh," said West. "Dallas, are you sleepy?"

Lesley looked beyond him to where Dallas nodded. She looked at the others apologetically. "I hope you'll excuse me, but when Dallas is ready to go to sleep, he goes to sleep."

"I'll take him," said West, getting to his feet. He swung Dallas up into his arms, and the child put his cheek on West's shoulder.

"Why don't you put him in your old room, West?" suggested Harold.

Dallas looked at Christine. "Will you save my pumpkin pie?" he asked her sleepily.

"Of course, dear," she answered kindly. The smile she gave her son and grandson was slightly tilted. Lesley thought she saw tears in her eyes. "You can have it after your nap."

An hour later the group relaxed in Harold's study, the most informal room Lesley had seen thus far in the huge house. A television played softly in one corner and the men gathered around to watch a football game. Lesley and the other women sat in another furniture grouping across the room, talking.

Lesley wished she weren't having so much trouble keeping her eyes open.

West extricated himself from the group. "I'd better check on Dallas," he said.

"I'll go with you," Lesley offered immediately. She had to do something or she was going to sleep. He held out his hand and pulled her to her feet.

Upstairs, the halls were quiet. He led the way to his old room. Through the open door she could see Dallas begin to wiggle on the bed. "Looks like we got here just in time," she said softly.

"Shall we tell him now?" asked West. He sat on the edge of the bed and patted the mattress beside him.

Lesley joined him, a wary smile on her face. "You don't think we should wait until we get home?"

He pulled her close. "No," he answered. "It won't be easy at any time." He gave her a soft kiss, which turned quickly into a harder one.

Finally, she laid her head on his shoulder and sighed. He was right, and she was too thankful for their love and commitment to each other, for this wonderful family, to put up any sort of argument. "Okay."

"Tell me what?"

Neither of them noticed that Dallas had moved. Now he sat, Indian-style, staring at them interestedly. "Ya'll kiss a lot. Tell me what?" He crawled across the mattress to them.

West helped the boy onto his lap, keeping the other arm around Lesley. "You know that you're adopted, Dallas, that your mother picked you out when you were born, but she isn't your... birth mother," he said gently. When the child nodded he went on. "Maybe you don't quite understand exactly what that means yet, but if you ever have any questions, you know that your mother and I will always answer them truthfully, don't you?"

Dallas nodded again. His eyes widened in apprehension. Lesley recognized the expression. She felt a tightening around her heart. She closed her eyes for a second. *Please, God, don't let my baby be hurt by this.*

"Well, what we want to tell you is that—" he stopped and took a breath "—I am your real father. Your birth father. I didn't know about this until I met you and your mother."

Dallas blew out a breath and visibly relaxed. "Well, I know *that.*"

The adults stared at him.

"I don't think you understand—"

Dallas interrupted his mother. "I figured it out when I first saw that big picture downstairs."

West, confused, said, "What picture?"

"The one hanging over the fireplace in the living room. I asked Christine, and she said it was you when you were my age. It looks jus' like me. Exac'ly." *Exactly* was his new word. He seemed very pleased with himself at finding another place to use it.

Lesley started to chuckle, then to laugh. If there was a hint of hysteria in the laughter, her two men just smiled and waited. At last, she controlled the laughter with a happy sob. She placed both hands on Dallas's cheeks, mimicking his own gesture when he had something of importance to convey. "Do you think your little sister or brother will look like that, too?" she asked her son. Then she gazed at West, who was suddenly stunned. "We'll know in about seven months."

Dallas and West peppered her with jubilant questions and answers, which took several more minutes.

"Will we all be named Chadwick?" asked Dallas, who was in the process of being officially adopted by his father.

"All of us. We should go back downstairs and tell the others," West said, grinning proudly as he stood with Dallas still in the crook of his arm.

"I need to ask you one more thing," Dallas said to them. "And I don't know if they're gonna like it. Can I call Christine and Harold 'Granny' and 'Grandpa'?"

Lesley looked to West to answer that one. If ever two people didn't suggest *those* nicknames, they were Christine and Harold. On the other hand, they'd mellowed a lot since the wedding, she realized.

West chuckled. "I think it's a great idea. Why don't you ask them?"

* * * * *

MILLION DOLLAR SWEEPSTAKES

SWP-M96

The spirit of the holidays...
The magic of romance...
They both come together in

You're invited as Merline Lovelace and Carole Buck—
two of your favorite authors from two of your favorite
lines—capture your hearts with five joyous love stories
celebrating the excitement that happens when you
combine holidays and weddings!

Beginning in October, watch for

HALLOWEEN HONEYMOON by Merline Lovelace
(Desire #1030, 10/96)

Thanksgiving—
WRONG BRIDE, RIGHT GROOM by Merline Lovelace
(Desire #1037, 11/96)

Christmas—
A BRIDE FOR SAINT NICK by Carole Buck
(Intimate Moments #752, 12/96)

New Year's Day—
RESOLVED TO (RE)MARRY by Carole Buck
(Desire #1049, 1/97)

Valentine's Day—
THE 14TH...AND FOREVER by Merline Lovelace
(Intimate Moments #764, 2/97)

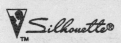

The collection of the year!
NEW YORK TIMES BESTSELLING AUTHORS

Linda Lael Miller
Wild About Harry

Janet Dailey
Sweet Promise

Elizabeth Lowell
Reckless Love

Penny Jordan
Love's Choices

and featuring
Nora Roberts
The Calhoun Women

This special trade-size edition features four of the wildly popular titles in the Calhoun miniseries together in one volume—a true collector's item!

Pick up these great authors and a chance to win a weekend for two in New York City at the Marriott Marquis Hotel on Broadway! We'll pay for your flight, your hotel—even a Broadway show!

Available in December at your favorite retail outlet.

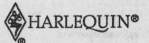
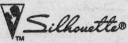

Silhouette
Yours Truly has a brand-new look!

Beginning in January 1997, Yours Truly will be sporting a
brand-new look. Be sure to look for us as we continue to
bring you fabulous stories to carry you into the
New Year with a smile on your face:

ME? MARRY *YOU?*
by Lori Herter

HEIRESS SEEKING PERFECT HUSBAND
by Maris Soule

Truly fun and contemporary, Yours Truly is filled
with stories you don't want to miss!

YOURS TRULY™

*Love-when you
least expect it.*

Available this January, wherever retail books are sold.

As seen on TV!
Free Gift Offer

With a Free Gift proof-of-purchase from any Silhouette® book,
you can receive a beautiful cubic zirconia pendant.

This gorgeous marquise-shaped stone is a genuine cubic
zirconia—accented by an 18" gold tone necklace.

(Approximate retail value $19.95)

Send for yours today...
compliments of ▼ *Silhouette*®
TM

To receive your free gift, a cubic zirconia pendant, send us one original proof-of-
purchase, photocopies not accepted, from the back of any Silhouette Romance™,
Silhouette Desire®, Silhouette Special Edition®, Silhouette Intimate Moments®
or Silhouette Yours Truly™ title available in August, September, October, November and
December at your favorite retail outlet, together with the Free Gift Certificate, plus a
check or money order for $1.65 U.S./$2.15 CAN. (do not send cash) to cover postage and
handling, payable to Silhouette Free Gift Offer. We will send you the specified gift. Allow
6 to 8 weeks for delivery. Offer good until December 31, 1996 or while quantities last.
Offer valid in the U.S. and Canada only.

Free Gift Certificate

Name: _____

Address: _____

City: _____ State/Province: _____ Zip/Postal Code: _____

Mail this certificate, one proof-of-purchase and a check or money order for postage
and handling to: SILHOUETTE FREE GIFT OFFER 1996. In the U.S.: 3010 Walden
Avenue, P.O. Box 9077, Buffalo NY 14269-9077. In Canada: P.O. Box 613, Fort Erie,
Ontario L2Z 5X3.

084-KMD-R

Your very favorite Silhouette miniseries
characters now have a BRAND-NEW story in

Brought to you by:

LINDA
HOWARD

DEBBIE
MACOMBER

LINDA
TURNER

LINDA HOWARD celebrates the holidays with a **Mackenzie**
wedding—once Maris regains her memory, that is....

DEBBIE MACOMBER brings **Those Manning Men** and
The Manning Sisters home for a mistletoe marriage as
a single dad finally says "I do."

LINDA TURNER brings **The Wild West** alive as
Priscilla Rawlings ties the knot at the Double R Ranch.

Three BRAND-NEW holiday love stories...by romance fiction's
most beloved authors.

Available in November at your favorite retail outlet.

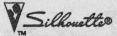

You're About to Become a

Privileged Woman

Reap the rewards of fabulous free gifts and benefits with proofs-of-purchase from Silhouette and Harlequin books

Pages & Privileges™

It's our way of thanking you for buying our books at your favorite retail stores.

Pages & Privileges™

**Harlequin and Silhouette—
the most privileged readers in the world!**

For more information about Harlequin and Silhouette's PAGES & PRIVILEGES program call the Pages & Privileges Benefits Desk: 1-503-794-2499

Silhouette®